"I just really, really…like you.…"

That made her feel a whole lot of things that were dangerous for her to be feeling.

Then he glanced up from his study of their hands intertwined and gazed into her eyes for a moment before he leaned just an inch or two closer, clearly aiming to kiss her.

But instead he paused, waiting as if tonight he wouldn't do it unless she met him halfway, unless she let him know that it was something she wanted him to do.

She wished she didn't. But wishing didn't make it so. She wanted him to kiss her so badly that she couldn't keep herself from drifting an inch or two forward herself, raising her chin almost imperceptibly but enough to give permission.

Permission he didn't hesitate to accept…

Dear Reader,

Flint Fortune grew up with a bad opinion of marriage. In spite of that, he was crazy enough to try it once himself, with disastrous results. Since then he's been convinced that marriage and family are not for him.

Jessie Hunt-Myers is a young widow who doubts that any man will ever be interested in taking on her and the four small children she's raising on her own.

During the past six months, the tides seem to be turning for all of the Fortune family of Red Rock, Texas, and while Flint may think he's not included in that, when he meets Jessie he can't be so sure. But four–count them–four kids? That's a whole lot to take on. And Flint just isn't altogether sure he can do it. The problem is, he also doesn't know how he's going to walk away from the most wonderful woman he's ever met.

I hope you enjoy this final installment in *The Fortunes of Texas: Lost...and Found.* I know I enjoyed writing it.

Happy summer reading!

Victoria Pade

FORTUNE FOUND

VICTORIA PADE

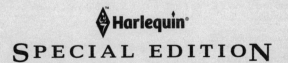

Harlequin®

SPECIAL EDITION

Special thanks and acknowledgment to Victoria Pade for her contribution to The Fortunes of Texas: Lost…and Found continuity.

ISBN-13: 978-0-373-65601-1

FORTUNE FOUND

Copyright © 2011 by Harlequin Books S.A.

Recycling programs
for this product may
not exist in your area.

www.Harlequin.com

Printed in U.S.A.

Books by Victoria Pade

VICTORIA PADE

is a *USA TODAY* bestselling author of numerous romance novels. She has two beautiful and talented daughters—Cori and Erin—and is a native of Colorado, where she lives and writes. A devoted chocolate lover, she's in search of the perfect chocolate-chip cookie recipe. For information about her latest and upcoming releases, and to find recipes for some of the decadent desserts her characters enjoy, log on to www.vikkipade.com.

Chapter One

"Iss him! Iss him! Iss Fwint, Mama!"

The announcement came from Jessica Hunt-Myers's excited three-year-old son, Adam, when he dashed to the open bathroom door, poked his head in, then dashed out again.

"Let me guess," Jessie said to her sister, her tone holding no shortage of suspicion. "That phone call a little while ago was from Flint Fortune, saying he was on his way. *That's* why you stopped me from sanding the baseboards, rushed me into your bathroom and gave me this sudden makeover."

Jessie stood with her hips resting on the counter-top that surrounded the sink, facing her sister, Kelsey. Kelsey was wielding a fluffy blush brush and applying the powder to Jessie's face much the way they'd played dress up with their mother's makeup when they were little girls.

Kelsey gave her a wide-eyed smile. "This really is new stuff that I just wanted you to try because I thought you'd like it. And that clip *does* look better in your hair than it did in mine," she said innocently.

Jessie rolled her eyes, not buying the innocent act for a second. "Kelsey…" she groaned. "First you try to match me with a guy you like yourself—the guy you ended up with—and now you're trying to push his brother?"

Kelsey shrugged. "I kept the first one for myself. It seems only fair that I find you someone else to make it up to you," she joked.

The first one had been Cooper Fortune and after unsuccessfully attempting to put Jessie together with Coop, Kelsey had succumbed to her own attraction to the man. They were now engaged, raising Cooper's six-month-old son, Anthony, and had moved into the house next door to Jessie's.

The house was in need of extensive remodeling, which was the reason Jessie and Adam—the youngest of Jessie's four children—were at Kelsey's house late that Sunday afternoon. Jessie was helping with some of the work.

The renovation was also why Cooper's brother, Flint, was scheduled for an extended stay in Kelsey and Coop's guest room.

An extended stay that was apparently about to begin.

"I don't need—or *want*—to be fixed up with anyone," Jessie said emphatically.

"It's been two years since Peter died, Jess," Kelsey cajoled gently.

"Two years, eleven days, three hours."

Kelsey shook her head sadly. "And you need more in your life to distract you from still counting the days. The hours."

"More in my life?" Jessie said with a laugh. "I have *four* kids, Kelsey. Mom and Dad retired to move in with me and lend me a hand because I have *so much* in my life—"

"Your kids will grow up, Mom and Dad will decide to travel or get a place in a retirement community the way they talked about before. And then where will you be, Jess? Alone—that's where."

"With a bathroom all to myself and a house that actually stays clean for five minutes and the possibility that I might never again run out of cookies…" Jessie said in a dreamy tone of voice, making light of the bleak picture her sister was painting.

"Alone," Kelsey repeated direly.

"Ella is seven. Braden and Bethany are four. Adam is only three. It'll be a long, long time before I have to worry about that."

"But don't you want someone for yourself again now?" Kelsey persisted. "Pete would have wanted—"

"Oh, don't pull that one! I hate it when people say what Pete would have wanted."

"Okay, then he *wouldn't* have wanted you to end up old and alone," Kelsey insisted, reversing it.

"I'm not ready," Jessie said definitively. "And when I am, it will happen. *Without* your beating the bushes for a man for me."

"I haven't been beating the bushes. I just think that

sometimes fate presents opportunities and I know that without a push, you won't see what's right in front of you. Even though Flint is pretty hard to overlook—or didn't you notice how hot he is?"

"Are you having second thoughts?" Jessie goaded her sister, turning the tables to distract her.

It didn't work.

"No! It's *because* I'm so in love with Coop that I want the same thing for you. And because I've learned firsthand that these Fortune men are men worth having and I want you to have a man who's worth having. The way Pete was."

"You can't be sure that Flint Fortune is a man worth having just based on his brother. You barely know Flint himself."

That particular member of the famed Fortune family of Texas didn't live in their small town of Red Rock where so many other Fortunes did, so he was a stranger to both Kelsey and Jessie. A stranger who had come into town when suspicions arose that an abandoned baby might have been his son, the baby who had proved instead to be Coop's child. The fact that Flint Fortune was inclined now to help out his brother and spend a little time with the rest of the family he didn't seem close to, didn't mean he was any less of a stranger to Kelsey or to Jessie.

"Okay, maybe I don't really know much about him," Kelsey admitted. "But I know he's Coop's brother and a really, *really,* hot guy…"

"*Hot* is not enough to sell him," Jessie persisted.

But it was the one thing Jessie couldn't argue because it was the plain and simple truth. She'd met Flint at the party Lily Fortune had had at the Double Crown ranch to introduce baby Anthony to the whole clan. And while Jessie might not have become wide-eyed with instant hero-worship of Flint the way her youngest son had, she had certainly not been able to overlook how impossibly attractive the man was.

"And no matter how *hot* he is," she said to her sister, "I'm not in the market for *any* man."

Not that she had so much as the most remote hope that any man was likely to want a widow with four small children. And if she allowed for the possibility of having a man in her life and then got rejected by him *because* of her kids? That just wasn't a door she wanted opened. For her kids or for herself.

Plus rejection also equaled loss, and putting herself or her kids in line for suffering the loss of another man was also not—absolutely *not*—something she was going to do.

"Adam already thinks Flint hangs the moon…" Kelsey reminded in a singsong intended to tempt Jessie.

"Well, Flint *doesn't* hang the moon," Jessie responded in the same singsong. "He's just a guy in a world full of guys who I don't have the time or the inclination to mess around with."

"Look at yourself," Kelsey implored, stepping back, taking Jessie by the shoulders and turning her to face the mirror. "You look fantastic. Don't wait around until the lines come in and everything starts to sag and droop and shrivel up—"

"Thank you so much for *that* image of my future."

Jessie scowled, then craned her head to get a better glimpse of her sable-colored brown hair in the back. "One way or another, this hair clip hurts and I don't want it," she said, taking it out and shaking her hair so it fell free around her shoulders.

"The blush is nice, though, isn't it?" Kelsey said. "It's a little sparkly."

Jessie studied her face more closely in the mirror, wondering if her slightly pale skin or her brown eyes or her maybe-a-little-too-straight-and-thin nose really were good enough to get her another man...

But she shied away from even the thought of that and judged the blush alone. "Yeah, it's nice." Because it did accentuate her high cheekbones and give her a healthy glow.

"Now tuck your T-shirt into your jeans so your butt shows," Kelsey said, as if that simple admission that the blush was nice had encouraged her.

"Kelsey—"

"Come on. Those aren't your best jeans, but you still have a good rear end that can *almost* be seen in them." Kelsey began to tuck in the back of Jessie's T-shirt.

"Will you stop?" Jessie protested.

"No, I won't!" Kelsey decreed. "It's bad enough that you're wearing a big old T-shirt with a slogan on it, at least tuck it in."

"I beg your pardon! The kids gave me this T-shirt for Mother's Day and I like it," she said, looking fondly down at the front of it where a picture of all four kids mugging for a camera stared back at her from beneath lettering that proclaimed her the *World's Greatest Mom.*

"I know—I helped them pick it out. But you were supposed to *sleep* in it, not wear it outside of the house," Kelsey chastised.

"I can't just *sleep* in it. One of them might think I'm not proud of it."

It was Kelsey who rolled her eyes this time. "Just tuck it in at least, and come out and say hello to Flint."

"I don't suppose I have a choice because he's out there."

Well, she *did* have a choice about tucking in or not tucking in the T-shirt. And even though she assured herself that she was only doing it so she didn't look like a slob, she unzipped her jeans, tugged the tails of the shirt down inside them and then zipped them up again.

"Happy?" she asked her sister as if she'd only done it to appease Kelsey.

But while Jessie had tucked in her T-shirt, Kelsey had produced a hairbrush from somewhere and was holding that out to her. "Now put this through your hair and I try this lipstick—"

"No lipstick!" Jessie refused. But she took the brush and swiped it through her hair just so she was presentable. Certainly not to impress Flint Fortune or any other man.

And for that same reason, just before she followed Kelsey out of the bathroom, she took one final glance at herself in the mirror.

And regretted that she hadn't worn jeans that were slightly less baggy.

And a T-shirt that wasn't so oversize she *should* only be using it for pajamas.

But truly, it was just because she didn't like to meet anyone when she looked sloppy.

It had nothing to do with Flint Fortune himself.

Truly.

* * *

"See, Mom? I tol' you—iss Fwint!"

"Yes, I see—F-*l*-int," Jessie answered her son, correcting Adam's pronunciation, before she focused her attention on the new arrival after Kelsey had welcomed him with a hug.

"Hi, Flint," Jessie greeted the man whose presence seemed to command the living room where he stood, a full five-feet-eleven inches of pure masculinity.

"Hi. Jessie, right? You're Kelsey's sister?"

"She's my sister all right," Kelsey confirmed with great enthusiasm.

But to Jessie the question had sounded like a shot-in-the-dark guess and she thought that that indicated that she hadn't made much of an impression on him.

He, however, was every bit as impossibly attractive as she recalled from the party.

Unlike her late-husband's boy-next-door looks, Flint Fortune had a swarthy, staggering handsomeness. His hair and eyes were brown, like Pete's. But unlike the lighter shades that her dearly departed husband had sported, Flint's hair was a deep, rich, bittersweet-chocolate brown, and his eyes were also much, much darker—the color of espresso with flecks of gold. Unusual, penetrating eyes that somehow seemed to hint at hidden depth in the man himself.

Although she had no idea why she was noticing that.

It was Kelsey's fault, Jessie decided, for putting thoughts of how hot this man was in her head.

But there was certainly no denying that he was hot. Hotter than hot. Above those unusual eyes were straight brows and a square forehead that was the perfect canvas to sport his slightly wavy, eminently touchable-looking hair. His nose was straight and well-shaped above full, provocative lips, and he had just the faintest dip in a chin that was hammocked between sharply drawn, granite jaws.

Add to that striking face broad shoulders that were barely contained by the Western-style shirt he was wearing with the sleeves rolled up to reveal muscular forearms and somehow-sexy wrists; narrow hips and long, thick legs that did great justice to the pair of jeans he was wearing, and there was no question that this was a formidably good-looking man.

But that didn't change a thing as far as Jessie was concerned.

"Fwint has cowboy boots like me!" Adam announced, obviously taking in every inch of Flint. Much the way his mother just had, although she'd missed the boots. "Mine are home. I wanna go get 'em!"

"Not right now you won't," Jessie intervened.

"But I wanna wear 'em!"

"You can't wear cowboy boots with your shorts. You can wear them another day, when it's cooler," Jessie said, eliciting a frown from her youngest before he bent over to study Flint's feet more closely.

"Will my feets get big as Fwint's feets?"

For no reason Jessie could fathom that made her wonder what Flint's naked feet looked like. Which was not only totally bizarre, but seemed like something too personal for her to be thinking about at all and she curbed her wandering thoughts.

She also decided to curb her overzealous son who had risen from his close scrutiny to stand with one arm wrapped around the big man's left leg and the side of his tennis shoe-clad foot against Flint's to compare them.

"I'm sorry," Jessie muttered, dragging Adam away from the grip that was more familiar than he should have been having with any stranger and firmly holding him against the front of her own thighs. "This must be some kind of new phase. He's never been so…" She wasn't sure how to say that her son seemed enthralled with this man. She settled on "…so taken with anyone before."

"I like 'im," Adam announced matter-of-factly. "I wanna do what he doos."

"Seems like Adam has decided you're his role model, Flint," Kelsey contributed with a pointed glance at Jessie, inspiring another eye roll from Jessie.

But undaunted, Kelsey said, "Coop is working in the basement. Jess, why don't you and Adam take Flint up and show him the room that'll be his while he's here so I can go get my other favorite Fortune man and tell him his brother is finally back?"

Jessie shot her sister an I'll-get-you-for-this glance. But she couldn't refuse the request without appearing rude, so she had to concede.

Refocusing on Flint's cover-model face, she said, "What will eventually be the actual guest room is down here. But right now it's full of paint cans and supplies, so Kelsey was thinking you could take the extra bedroom upstairs."

"I'll show you," Adam offered, breaking free of his mother's grip to run for the stairs in the entryway.

"I guess we should follow our leader," Flint said with a sexy half smile, apparently amused by her son.

"If we don't he's liable to drag you upstairs himself," Jessie said.

"There's not much to him, that could do him some damage," Flint joked. Then he leaned over and picked up the suitcase he must have brought in with him, and said, "After you."

Had her sister not pointed out the fact that she wasn't wearing her most flattering jeans, Jessie was convinced that the way her rear end looked in them wouldn't have crossed her mind. Or the fact that she had Flint Fortune directly behind her on the stairs.

Now she was far more conscious of where his eyes might be as they climbed the steps. And of what he might be thinking if he was at all interested in checking her out—which he probably wasn't. But if he was, could he tell her butt wasn't bad despite the baggy jeans?

But those were not thoughts she wanted to be having. And trying to elude them, she finished the second half of the stairs at a quicker pace.

Adam was waiting for them at the landing, his father's brown eyes watching eagerly for Flint.

The moment Flint reached the top, Adam said, "Iss over here," and made a dash for the bedroom beside the nursery where Anthony was napping.

Jessie and Flint again trailed her son into the small bedroom that had yet to be decorated but contained the necessities—a double bed, a nightstand complete with a lamp and a dresser upon which was an old television set.

"We live there!" Adam announced excitedly. He was standing at one of the bedroom's two windows and pointing to the house next door.

"Ah, right. Coop mentioned that."

Jessie appreciated that Flint indulged the little boy by setting his suitcase down and joining Adam at the window.

"See?" Adam said when Flint got there. "Tha's my mom's window. You can see 'er when she puts on her 'jamas and stuff."

Out of the mouths of babes…

It was an innocent-enough comment, so there wasn't anything to actually be embarrassed by. And yet Jessie felt some heat rise in her cheeks. Possibly because she was picturing the kind of scene Adam was unwittingly portraying.

Or possibly because it seemed as if Flint might be, too, because he turned a disarmingly devilish smile to her.

"That's why we pull our shades when we undress, Adam," Jessie lectured. "So no one *can* see us when we put on our pajamas."

"But you could wave to each other," Adam persisted. "Cuz wookit, tha's yur room, Mama, I kin see it!"

"Yes, that's my room," Jessie acknowledged.

"And we'll be sure to wave to each other. Every night," Flint assured, barely suppressing a grin.

"Oh, definitely," Jessie agreed as if she, too, could joke about it when the truth was that she was having a silly schoolgirl image of peering at the handsome man just across the way.

"An' wookit down there," Adam said then, oblivious of the exchange between the adults. "Tha's my gramma and grampa cookin' on the barber-cue, and tha's Ella an' Braden an' Beth'ny playin' wis the hose—you kin see them all, too."

"I can," Flint said.

"And if Gramma and Grampa are cooking that means we'd better get home for dinner," Jessie said, using the information to make her escape.

"Can Fwint come?"

"Aunt Kelsey has other plans for Flint's dinner tonight."

"Can I come back *after* dinner?" the tiny child asked hopefully.

"After dinner you need a bath, so no. You'll see Flint again soon."

"As I understand it, we're all going to be working on the house this week, buddy, so we'll probably see a lot of each other."

Jessie recognized the expressions that crossed her son's face as he decided whether to throw a tantrum or be appeased. In the end he drew an exaggerated breath, sighed it out with great effect and said a very reluctant, "Okay."

"Come on, let's get going," Jessie said, seizing the moment before he changed his mind and threw the tantrum anyway.

"And Adam?" Flint added as the little boy trudged from the window to his mother. "I'll be wearing tennis shoes like yours tomorrow, so don't worry about the boots."

Jessie laughed lightly at that and said, "Thanks, that saves me a fight tomorrow morning."

"I thought it might," Flint said with yet another smile, this one understanding and yet still so engaging.

Engaging enough that a split-second elapsed while Jessie stared into that smile, into those unique eyes of his and forgot everything.

Then Adam yanked her back to reality by taking her

hand and tugging her downward while he stood on his tip-toes to whisper, "He called me *buddy*. Tha' means we're frien's."

"That is what it means," Jessie confirmed, appreciating that Flint had taken some care with her son's feelings. Telling herself that that was all she was appreciating about the man.

And all she *intended* to appreciate about him.

Chapter Two

Flint woke Monday morning to the sound of children's voices outside, a baby fussing in the next room, water running somewhere nearby and a sprinkler *whoosh-whoosh-whooshing* in the distance.

Definitely not the quiet of his apartment on the outskirts of Denver.

Then his brother Cooper's voice drifted to him from somewhere close by, reminding him that he was in Texas. In Red Rock.

Where his mother was born and raised. Where a chunk of his extended family lived. Where his mother had brought him, his two brothers and his sister to visit growing up—usually because she'd wanted to get rid of her kids while she went on yet another honeymoon, or because she needed to finagle money out of some of that extended family between husbands or jobs or cities or any of the other flights of fancy that were always in play with Cindy Fortune.

Flint opened his eyes and recognized the tidy spare bedroom of the house his brother had just moved into. Where he was taking a slight hiatus from his own work to help fix up the place and spend some time with Coop, his newly discovered son, Anthony, and new fiancée, Kelsey, and with he and Coop's other brother Ross and their sister, Frannie, who also lived in Red Rock.

He'd be spending time with some of the other extended family, too, but for a change that didn't strike him as such a bad thing.

In the last five months the Fortune family had seen a lot of turmoil that was hopefully beginning to settle down. Turmoil that still came with a whole lot of questions that had yet to be answered because the current head of the family—his Uncle William—had suffered a head injury in a car accident and remained in the throes of amnesia, unable to answer those questions.

But surprisingly to Flint, in the course of all the madness, he and his siblings had learned that they really weren't considered the black sheep of the Fortune family the way they'd always thought they were. That they were actually thought of as valued members of the group in spite of their mother and the haphazard way she'd raised them. In spite of the fact that none of them had been quite as brilliantly successful as their cousins.

So for once Flint was happy to be in Red Rock, even if all the noise had cost him his last half hour of sleep.

Because it was impossible for him to doze off with the racket outside, he conceded to it, sat up and swung his feet to the floor.

Which left him facing the window aimed at the

house next door. The house young Adam had pointed out to him yesterday when he'd first gotten here. Jessie's house.

That had to be where all the voices were coming from.

For the sake of decency, Flint dragged on his jeans from the day before and a white undershirt. Then he stood and went to the window. The drapes left a gap that gave him a view of the other house even from bed. Now he used a single index finger to nudge them open a few inches more so he could better see out.

Yep, a whole passel of kids were running around in the backyard, where it looked like parts for a swing set or a jungle gym were being delivered.

Flint couldn't have cared less about that. But he stayed at the window, his gaze drifting up to the one directly across from his.

Jessie's curtains were open this morning. They hadn't been when he'd checked last night before he'd gone to bed before closing his own drapes as far as they would go. But there was no sign of Kelsey's sister, then or now.

He had to laugh a little, though, when he thought about what young Adam had said the day before and the fact that those curtains had been so steadfastly closed last night to ensure that he hadn't been able to see Jessie put on her pajamas, or even just smile and wave when she saw him.

Too bad.

He wouldn't have minded getting a glimpse of that petite body, with the great rear end that had tantalized him all the way up the stairs and the hint of firm breasts hidden beneath that oversize T-shirt.

The weird thing was that he also wouldn't have minded just seeing her wave to him. And for *that* he had no explanation.

What was he, some schoolboy hoping for just a look at the girl next door? Just a raise of her hand to acknowledge him?

He hadn't felt like that since he was thirteen. He'd actually stood there for at least half an hour last night hoping she would appear. And here he was again this morning.

She *was* something to look at, he told himself as consolation for how dumb it seemed.

Not that he hadn't seen—up close and personal—plenty of women who were something to look at. But a pretty woman was always something to look at. And Kelsey's sister? She was more than just pretty. A lot more.

When he'd first seen her yesterday, he'd recalled, instantly, the first moment he'd seen her.

She was the woman from Lily's party who had caught his eye over and over again, long before he'd finally been introduced to her.

Jessie—he'd barely learned her name and he hadn't had the chance for more than that at the time.

Then all of a sudden yesterday, there she'd been again, in the living room downstairs.

She *was* lovely. Downright beautiful, actually. Even in baggy jeans and that *World's Greatest Mom* T-shirt. Beautiful, but in an approachable kind of way. Natural and artless. And without any indication that she was even aware of her looks.

She had the silkiest hair he'd ever seen—chestnut brown and so shiny that it glistened as it fell to below her shoulders around a face that no man could ignore. Her skin was fresh and flawless, interrupted by only a small, adorable dot of a beauty mark just below the corner of her left eye.

And those eyes, big, round, cocoa-brown, they had the softest look to them. They glimmered a little—they were almost dewy. He'd had trouble glancing away from them.

Until his own gaze had slid down her straight, thin, well-shaped nose to those lush, exquisite lips. Slightly full but not too full. Petal pink. Just the right shape. Perfect whether she was smiling or talking or doing nothing at all with them. Perfect for kissing...

Not that he'd ever know if *that* was true, he reprimanded himself, shoving aside the thought by altering his view from her bedroom window to her backyard again.

Four kids.

Four!

A mom—however beautiful—who had been widowed somehow and left to raise them on her own. That was a situation shouting for him to stay away.

He was happy for his own three siblings—all married or engaged. But for himself? Marriage wasn't in the cards.

He'd tried it once, and once was enough. More than enough to confirm what he'd seen of marriage growing up and watching his mother do it again and again. Complicated and difficult and costly. Something that could too easily deteriorate into a very, very ugly situation— that was what marriage was to him, and as far as he was concerned, it didn't have anything to recommend it.

And the fact that Jessie had four kids?

Flint wasn't a kid person. One of the worst pieces of news he'd ever received in his life had come last month when word had gotten to him that Anthony might be his. He hadn't had the foggiest idea what he was going to do if that was true. And he'd never experienced the kind of relief he'd known when the baby had turned out to be Cooper's instead.

I'm just not dad material, he thought, remembering Kelsey's comment about how Adam had chosen him as a role model and not even feeling as if he could be that. He didn't have any idea how to be either of those things. How could he when his own father had barely had anything to do with him, when none of his mother's other men—husbands or not—had ever hung around long enough to be either of those to him? When he hadn't spent enough time with the Fortunes to have found that in Red Rock either?

Plus he liked his freedom. He liked coming and going as he pleased. He was enjoying his life the way it was now and he didn't want to change anything.

And when it came to women? There was no shortage of them—never had been. Not even when he made it clear that he had a strict no-strings policy. That he liked to keep things light.

Which didn't mean kids. Or the extra responsibility, the extra burden of worrying about those kids ending up feeling the way he and his sister and brothers had felt every time another man had come into their mother's—and consequently their—lives. Every time they even began to get accustomed to those same men and then watched them walk out the door.

It was something he never wanted to inflict on any child, let alone four of them.

So Jessie was a no-go for him. However beautiful she was, with four kids who could end up getting hurt in the shuffle he'd learned so well as a child himself, she was strictly, totally, completely, one-hundred-percent off-limits, regardless of how beautiful she was. Or how doe-soft her eyes were. Or how kissable her lips might be, or how much he'd wanted to reach up and run his fingertips over her cheek to find out if her skin was as smooth as it looked...

Then, suddenly, there she was—in the yard with all her kids.

And just as suddenly all those kids seemed to fade into the background as he honed in on her as if she were out there alone, her hair drinking in the morning sunshine and reflecting it.

She was wearing better-fitting jeans today, with a tank top tucked into the jeans. And when she leaned over to check a tag on whatever it was that had been delivered, her well-shaped backside was impossible for him not to look at.

Flint's hand actually tingled with the urge to cup that great little bum, and suddenly being a good role model was the last thing on his mind. Only Jessie was. And the fact that in just a while she was scheduled to come over here and work...

Knock it off! he commanded himself, refocusing his eyes, making sure his view again took in those four kids running around, climbing on things, making a ruckus.

She has four kids, he told himself once more, firmly, sternly, determined to brand it into his brain so that he never lost sight of it.

But then she stood up straight again, turned enough to be in profile, slipped her hands into the rear pockets of those jeans and this time it was the sweet, sweet swell of her breasts that made his hands ache to touch.

But it didn't matter, he swore to himself. She was a no-go.

And he meant it. If he had to dredge up every lousy memory he had of his own childhood to stick to it, that's what he'd do.

But one way or another he wasn't getting involved with The Mom Next Door.

"I don't think I know your last name—or is it Hunt, like Kelsey's?"

It was not easy for Jessie to be in her sister's laundry room, sharing the painting duties with Flint late Monday afternoon after he and Cooper had returned from buying supplies for that day's project.

The space was small—only big enough for a side-by-side washer and drier with enough room in front of them to open their front-loading doors. And if Flint had seemed to fill Kelsey's entire living room the day before with his mere presence, it was nothing compared to the laundry room.

In close quarters, alone, with a potently attractive man—how was she supposed to keep her mind on painting, let alone small talk?

There was nothing Jessie could do but try to make the best of it. And because Flint was going to be her sister's brother-in-law, she decided she might as well get to know him.

"I'm Hunt-Myers," Jessie answered, hoping it wasn't unduly belated and also hoping that the fact that she'd been climbing to sit cross-legged on the tarp covering the drier so she could paint the wall behind it offered a reason for the delay. "I hyphenated when I got married. I guess it was a way of maintaining some independence and then it stuck."

They'd begun painting at the door, gone in opposite directions but were now both working on the long wall behind the appliances. The lower half of the wall was tiled and so didn't need paint, and unlike Jessie, Flint was tall enough to reach the half above the appliances just by leaning over the washing machine.

He was dressed in a pair of old, ragged, torn jeans, and an equally as worn chambray shirt with the sleeves rolled to his elbows. They were clearly work clothes and yet they still managed to look good on him—and to accentuate his every asset. Assets that Jessie was all too aware of when his well-shaped rear end, or muscular jean-encased thighs, or broad shoulders or expansive chest were always mere inches away from her.

"What about you?" she countered. "You and Coop are both Fortunes, but you're Fortunes on your mother's side, aren't you?"

"We are," he said amiably. "My mother never took any of her husband's last names. Maybe she knew none of her marriages would last."

Beyond the fact that Cindy Fortune was not well thought of, Jessie knew nothing about Flint and Cooper's mother. But even though she was curious—especially about that comment about multiple marriages—it seemed beyond the realm of small talk to ask for details. So with the name-related questions answered, she opted for moving on.

"You live in Denver, right?" she said then.

"Right. Just outside of the city itself."

"Do you have a house or—"

"I rent an apartment. I like to have a home base, but not with roots that are too deep. If I end up with a neighbor I don't like, or the grass looks greener somewhere else, I want to be able to pack my stuff and move on without much fuss. That's what I grew up with, and I guess it stuck."

"The Fortune family are staples around here— ranchers, businessmen, philanthropists—they're pillars of the community. But you grew up rootless?"

"Oh, yeah," he answered with a mirthless laugh.

But again he didn't offer an explanation beyond that and again Jessie thought that to push him for more might be prying.

He didn't let there be an awkward silence, though, before he said, "What about you? Do you own the place next door?"

"I do," she answered, liking that he didn't put her in a position of quizzing him, that he asked questions of his own. Although she tried not to think that he might actually be interested in her, and told herself he was likely just being polite.

"Owning a house of our own was my late-husband's and my biggest goal when we got married," she went on. "It took us five years of saving, but we celebrated our fifth anniversary by moving into that house."

"And you're still there after how long?"

"Eight years."

"That's an eternity to me. You must be all about deep roots."

"Stability is important to me."

"And family, too, I'm guessing—because your parents live with you and now you have Kelsey right next door."

"You could definitely say I'm all about family," she confirmed. "I don't know what I would do without them."

"That's nice," he said just when she was wondering if he was approving or disapproving of her closeness to her family. But he sounded as if he honestly did think it was nice and she wondered if he regretted that he wasn't closer to his own family.

But again he kept their chat going by saying, "It was you who gave Coop the heads-up when this place became available, wasn't it?"

"It was. That's how it all came about so fast."

"And they're renting with an option to buy, right?"

"With the first three months rent-free because none of this work is being hired out."

"That's a big change for Coop, too—that putting down roots thing. But he seems really happy."

"I think he is. I know Kelsey is."

"Good for them!" Flint decreed. "And Kelsey is okay raising Anthony?"

"She is. I don't think she would love him any more if he were her own."

Jessie knew that Anthony was the product of an earlier relationship Cooper had had with a woman named Lulu. There were many questions about Anthony turning up in Red Rock at the same time Flint and Cooper's Uncle William had had his car accident in January. Ultimately Anthony had been linked to the Fortunes through a small gold medallion that had been draped around his blanket-cocooned little body by a fragile chain. A medallion that had been traced back to Cindy Fortune's children, narrowing the possibilities for Anthony's father to Cooper or Flint.

"I'm really glad it all worked out for them the way it did," Flint said. "It looks like Anthony will have a good home."

"Were you disappointed that he wasn't yours?" Jessie asked.

Flint laughed spontaneously. "No," he answered forcefully. "I was a wreck thinking he might be mine and wondering what I was going to do with him if he was. I can't even keep plants alive. Believe me, this was a much better way for things to turn out."

"What would you have done if he'd been yours?" Jessie ventured, challenging him just a bit.

He laughed again. "I probably would have cried like a baby myself," he joked.

Jessie smiled at the wall she was painting, amused by the thought of the man she'd been thinking of as super-macho quaking at the mere possibility that he might be a father.

"I would have stepped up," he said then, without hesitation, winning him points. "But I'm afraid poor Anthony would have suffered for it."

Jessie laughed at him. "Well, I know you travel for work and that would have made it a lot more compli-cated, so you're probably right—it's for the best that things ended up the way they did."

But what she didn't know was much about his work and that seemed like another avenue for conversation, so she said, "You're in sales, aren't you?"

"Buying and selling, yeah."

"What is it that you buy and sell?"

"I buy Western-themed arts and crafts and novelty items, and I sell them to gift shops and galleries and some private clients all across the country."

That piqued her interest. "When you say that you buy arts and crafts and novelty items, do you mean from manufacturers or—"

"I have accounts with some wholesale houses that bring up trinket-type things from Mexico. But whenever I can I buy from artists and craftsmen. I like to deal in the unique and original more than in the mass-produced stuff."

"Do you work for a company or something?"

"The business is mine. But *business* sounds more… I don't know, *corporate* than I am. I've just come up with a name—Fortune Fine Arts and Crafts—because I'm in the process of having a website set up so I can do more selling over the internet. But really, I'm just a middleman—I hunt down stuff to sell, usually buy it outright myself and then resell it at a profit. Or sometimes I find a gallery or shop that will let me place a piece there and if it sells, the money gets split three ways—between whoever produced it, whoever's shop or gallery it was sold from, and me."

"That would make you an agent or an artist's representative, then, wouldn't it?"

"Again, sounds a lot fancier than I am. What I am is an old-fashioned horse trader. Except that I don't deal in horses, I deal in brass sculptures of horses and kachina dolls and hand-sewn moccasins and tribal headdresses and authentic totem poles."

"Hmm. I never considered that there would be a market for tribal headdresses or totem poles."

"They aren't my best sellers, but they're fairly popular for decorating hunting and fishing lodges and hotels that want a rustic appeal."

"And I guess you can't call yourself a totem pole seller," she teased him a little.

"That's why we just say that I'm in sales," he concluded, pleasing her with the fact that he'd grasped her gentle gibe.

"Is the goal of the new website to reduce the amount of travel you have to do?" she asked.

"I guess potentially it could, but the traveling doesn't bother me. I don't have anything tying me down, and I like getting around, seeing the country. The life of a traveling salesman suits me."

Their painting met at the center of the wall behind the washer and drier then, and while Flint stepped back to survey their handiwork, Jessie used one final application of her roller to blend that meeting line seamlessly.

And with that, she sat back and looked around, too.

"That didn't take long," she admitted, thinking that the time had actually seemed to fly.

"Apparently we work well together," Flint said just as Adam burst through the door with an excited, "Hi, Fwint!"

"Hi, Adam," Flint greeted the three-year-old with a mirroring of Adam's enthusiasm. "Where've you been today?"

"He'ppin my grampa wis our new junger gym. We digged howes for plantin' the powes so it don't fauw over."

"They dug *holes* to cement the *poles* into the ground so the jungle gym doesn't *fall* over," Jessie translated. "Sometimes the L's come out and sometimes they just don't." Then to her son, she said, "What are you doing here now?"

Before Adam answered that Jessie heard the voice of her oldest daughter, Ella, calling for Adam.

"We're in the laundry room, El," Jessie called back.

The seven-year-old bounded in, much the way Adam had except rather than joyfully having discovered Flint, the much more serious Ella scowled at her brother. "Gramma said you could only come with me if you held my hand, and you didn't!"

"I had to find Fwint," Adam answered as if his sister should have known that.

"Ella, you remember Flint, don't you? Coop's brother?" Jessie interjected, both to remind her daughter of her manners and to avoid a fight between her oldest and youngest.

"I remember," was all Ella said to Flint because she was still more intent on wrangling with her brother. And to Adam she goaded, "*Fl*int. His name is *Fl*int."

"Okay, okay," Jessie said before war broke out. "What's up, El?"

"Gramma says it's almost dinnertime and she needs a pan she can't find to cook. Can you come home and show her where it is?"

"I think I can probably do that. We're finished here, aren't we?" Jessie said, trying not to analyze why she was sorry that that was true, and why she was also sorry to be pulled away so suddenly.

"Looks finished to me," Flint confirmed.

To Ella, Jessie said, "You can tell Gramma I'll come home as soon as I wash out these paint things."

"Come on, Adam, let's go," Ella said as if she'd just been given the upper hand.

"Ouw go wis Mama when she goes."

"Adam…" Ella said in the warning tone she always took when she was in the mode of oldest-child-as-boss.

This time it was Flint who stepped in before a fight broke out. To Jessie, he said, "I'll take care of the cleanup, go ahead and go home."

Jessie laughed. "Be careful. I'm the mother of four—I don't get offers for other people to cleanup too often and I never turn them down when I do."

That made him smile back at her—a wide grin that showed perfect white teeth and drew ever-so-appealing lines around the corners of his mouth. And the very fact that his smile made her flush was a phenomenon Jessie didn't want to delve into.

"Go," he urged with a nudge of that sexy, slightly dimpled chin.

"If you're sure…"

"I'm sure. It's nothing."

So he's not only hot, but he's also a nice guy, Jessie thought, remembering the previous day's conversation with her sister.

But that, too, wasn't something she should be caring about and she decided that before she started to actually like this guy, she'd better go home where she belonged.

"Okay, I'll take you up on that, then," she announced, scooting around on the drier so that she could get down.

But that set the tarp into motion and it began to slide, taking her with it until Flint lunged forward to catch her.

And in a split second Jessie found herself with Flint Fortune's handsome face scant inches from hers, his arms on either side of her, his hands flat against the tarp but so close to her rear end that she thought she could almost feel them.

And her own hands somehow clasped to his power-house shoulders to catch herself.

Wide-eyed, she stared into his dark eyes and wasn't quite sure whether it was the near fall from the drier or Flint that had stolen her breath. But one way or another, for a moment she was frozen there, so close that they could have kissed had either of them moved an inch.

And why *that* went through her mind, she had no idea.

"Mama?" Ella said with some shock in her voice.

It took Jessie a moment to remember herself, to breathe, to veer away from Flint and pull her hands from shoulders she was enjoying the feel of much too much...

"Whoops," she said feebly.

"Mama aw-most fawed off—tha's funny," Adam said with a giggle.

"Thanks for the catch," Jessie muttered, leaning as far back from Flint as she could.

But still he stayed where he was, anchoring the tarp, looking into her eyes, while a much more intimate smile slowly spread agile lips. So intimate that it made something skitter across the surface of Jessie's skin—a sensation she hadn't had in longer than she could remember.

"No problem," he said in a voice that had a deeper, almost sensual timbre.

Then he pushed off the drier and took hold of the tarp from behind her. "Okay, *now* slide off," he advised.

Under the watchful eye of two of her children, Jessie

did, wondering at the scowl that had come onto Ella's pretty, freckled face as the little girl glared at Flint as if he'd done something wrong.

"Okay, we better get going before Gramma sends more troops," Jessie said in a tone she hoped sounded normal. Inside, though, she was a jumble of excitement and confusion and something that seemed to remind her she was a woman—a feeling she hadn't experienced in a very, very long time.

As she guided her kids out of the laundry room she couldn't help glancing back just once because she thought she could feel Flint watching her.

He stood with his hips leaning against the front of the drier, his arms crossed over his wide chest. And he wasn't merely watching her—there was something else in those eyes that almost seemed appreciative...

Why that again set off that tingling-across-the-surface-of-her-skin feeling, that reminder that she was a woman, she didn't know.

She only knew that it needed to stop.

And it needed not to happen again.

She was a mother, first and foremost, and she couldn't let herself be distracted from that. She already had her hands full.

And yet just the thought of having her hands full made her mind wander back to the feel of Flint's rock-solid shoulders.

And whether she wanted to admit it or not, she'd liked the way they'd felt.

Chapter Three

Flint stood high atop his brother's roof early Tuesday morning. He was supposed to be checking for loose shingles. Instead he was so intent on watching Jessie cross from her backyard into Cooper's through the connecting gate that he was late in realizing that a car had pulled up in front of the house.

Only when Jessie had disappeared from sight was Flint's attention drawn in the opposite direction, just as his other brother Ross was getting out from behind the wheel.

"Hey, down there! This is a surprise!" Flint called.

No one had said anything about Ross coming by today, or about his bringing their uncle William and William's fiancée, Lily. But there they all were.

"I have some news," Ross yelled back as he closed the driver's side door.

Growing up, Ross, the oldest of Cindy's children had looked out for his siblings and in that same vein, Flint saw him making sure that the elderly couple got safely out of his car as Flint climbed down the ladder and met them at the front porch.

William and Lily were supposed to be married in January. The match between William and his late-cousin Ryan's widow had been kept quiet until they'd both felt the family could accept their relationship. The relationship that had come about despite the fact that William and Ryan had been close, despite the fact that Lily had adored her husband until his death six years before from a brain tumor. Two years ago, the also-widowed William and Lily had found their way to each other, and what had begun as a family connection turned into a friendship that had blossomed into love.

Their wedding had been set for January first—a New Year's Day celebration. But William had never made it to the church. There had been speculation that he'd run off with another woman, that he'd been kidnapped, that any number of things had caused him to leave Lily at the altar voluntarily or involuntarily. His car had been discovered days later, having gone off a road near the neighboring town of Haggerty, almost completely concealed in a wooded ravine. William was nowhere around.

For months it hadn't been known where he was, or whether he was dead or alive. Then, just a few weeks ago, he was located living on the streets in Haggerty, suffering from amnesia, not even aware of who he was.

Since being returned to Red Rock, to his family, to Lily—who had always believed William would return to her—he was getting better at recognizing the people who cared about him. And because he had a particular soft spot for Anthony—for no reason anyone could explain—Flint knew that whenever she got the chance, Lily liked to expose William to the baby in hope that something about Anthony was reaching William's deeply buried recollections and helping to draw them to the surface.

"I don't know what news you have, but it's good to see you all," Flint greeted the small group. "How are you feeling, Uncle William?"

"A little like I'm walking through a fog, but okay," the older man answered, still sounding slightly befuddled.

"I thought it might be better if I brought Lily and Uncle William with me rather than tell what I have to tell twice," Ross said then.

"Sure. Why don't we go inside?" Flint suggested, ushering the threesome up the porch steps and hollering "We have company," as he went in behind them all.

From upstairs came Coop, and from the kitchen at the rear of the house came Kelsey and the newly arrived Jessie.

And while Flint had no explanation for it, he only had eyes for Jessie, whom he said good morning to.

More greetings made the rounds and then Kelsey got everyone out to the picnic table in the backyard for coffee because no single section of the house could comfortably seat so many at once yet.

"I'm glad to see you back with us, Flint," William said as they all settled. "I do remember that you were leaving after Anthony's party for a business trip."

"And I'm glad to see that you know who I am," Flint teased his uncle.

With a nod in the direction of Jessie, William added, "And this beauty? She must be your wife?"

They *were* sitting beside each other—at Kelsey's suggestion. But Flint was slightly discouraged by this lapse in his uncle's recall.

"No, this is Jessie, Kelsey's sister," Flint explained as if it were no big deal that William had made the mistake. "I'm not married anymore."

As if to get past William's lapse, Lily jumped in then to ask where Anthony was.

"Coop just put him down for his morning nap," Kelsey answered. "But you can look in on him later if you want."

After a drink of his coffee, Ross took the lead. "I had a call from the police today," he began.

As a private detective, Ross was the family's closest link to law enforcement. He'd done all he could to try to find William when he was missing, as well as to look into the whereabouts of Lulu Carlton—Anthony's birth mother—for Cooper.

After having it confirmed that Anthony was Coop's son, Coop had done the math—he'd been involved with Lulu at the time Anthony would have been conceived. He hadn't had any idea that she was pregnant when they'd broken up and he'd left her in Minnesota, but Ross had discovered that she'd come to Texas.

Ross had also discovered that there had been a car accident near where William's car had gone off the road, on the same day William had disappeared, that a woman had been killed in that accident but that without identification, she was in the Haggerty morgue, listed as a Jane Doe.

The time lapse between when Jane Doe's accident

had been reported and when William's car had been discovered in the ravine days later had raised questions about whether the two incidents were related. No one had yet to answer those questions. But the coincidence had made Ross suggest that Cooper take a look at Jane Doe.

Sure enough, Coop had identified her as Lulu Carlton and provided his son's mother with a proper burial.

In the course of all that, Ross had had several dealings with state and local police, so it was no surprise that news coming through those same channels that involved the Fortune family would still go to Ross first.

"It seems," he was saying, "that the man who was working at the church as the groundskeeper in January was arrested for stealing a car and robbing a convenience store in Dallas a couple of days ago. His name is Charlie something-or-other. He wasn't alone, he had that Courtney woman with him—the one who brought Anthony to Max Allen—"

"Max Allen?" William asked, obviously lost.

Lily placed a reassuring hand over William's where it rested on the picnic table. "Remember you met him—he's Kirsten's brother?"

"Oh, that's right—that pretty girl my son Jeremy is going to marry. Max is her brother."

"Right," Ross confirmed. And apparently because William was drawing a blank, he explained what everyone else knew. "Courtney was Max Allen's old girlfriend. She showed up on his door with Anthony, saying he was Max's baby. Max didn't believe her, and it was because he brought Anthony to the attention of the authorities that we figured out that Anthony belongs to Coop."

"Ah," William said.

Because the older man seemed to have grasped that, Ross continued. "Police in Dallas came down pretty hard on both the church's former groundskeeper and this Courtney, looking for prior bad acts. Courtney broke down, gave enough information for the cops to use as leverage with the groundskeeper and—between the two of them—got the whole story. Apparently the groundskeeper found Anthony on the back doorstep of the church on what would have been the wedding day."

"And all this time we've been thinking that Anthony must have been in the accident with Lulu? That someone took him from the scene?" Coop said.

Ross shrugged. "No one knew where else he might have come from."

"But now it seems as if Lulu left him at the church?" Flint asked.

"We're thinking that maybe she saw the announcement of Uncle William and Lily's wedding somewhere, and thought that if she left him there that day, one of us would find him. That when we saw the medallion strung around him, we'd figure he belonged with us."

"But none of us *did* find him," Coop put in.

"So the groundskeeper took him," Ross went on, "and pawned Anthony off on this Courtney woman. She actually got attached to the baby, which was why she wanted to make sure he got to someone she thought might do right by him when it occurred to her that she couldn't keep him herself. That was when she went to Max Allen."

"And if I'm remembering right," Kelsey interjected, "First Courtney claimed that Anthony belonged to her and Max, then her story changed and she swore Anthony was her son with the groundskeeper."

"Right. But like I said, Max Allen got suspicious," Ross repeated. "And thanks to that and the medallion that these two less-than-upstanding citizens didn't take from Anthony, we were able to do the DNA test that connected him with Coop."

"We're so lucky this worked out the way it did," Coop said, choking up.

"It could have been so much worse," Kelsey said.

"But he ended up with the two of you," Flint reminded to soothe his brother and Kelsey's fears before they got unduly out of control with what might have been.

"Anthony ended up with his family," William confirmed victoriously. "That's all that matters."

"That and that we have you safely back, too," Lily put in, squeezing William's hand on the picnic table.

"Even if my memory is full of more holes than Swiss cheese," William joked.

They all laughed at that before assuring the older man that everything would come back in time—what Flint knew was just wishful thinking at that point.

Then, to Kelsey, Lily said, "We shouldn't keep you when you have so much work to do. Maybe we could just take that little peek at Anthony while he's sleeping and we'll get out of your way."

"I know I could use a peek at him," Coop said, still sounding unnerved by the thought of the complicated path his son had taken to get to him.

As everyone stood up from the picnic table, Kelsey turned to Flint and said, "Don't get back on the roof. I have jobs for you to do with Jessie today."

That brought a jab of Jessie's elbow into Kelsey's ribs that made Flint wonder if Jessie was unhappy with the prospect of working side by side with him.

But as Jessie began to gather empty coffee cups to take into the house, he hoped that that wasn't the case.

And not just because the morning sunshine glistened off her hair like spun copper.

But because as home repairs went, doing them side by side with her took all the chore out of it for him.

"When I says g'night to my grampa I kisses his cheek. But Grampa says that when other mens says g'night they pro'bly shakes han's."

And with that explanation, Adam held out his tiny hand for Flint to shake.

Jessie watched Flint fight to keep from laughing, smiling instead as he accepted Adam's outstretched hand and shook it. "Good night, Adam. Sleep tight."

"Tha's what my mama says," Adam exclaimed before he ran off to join his brother, sisters and grandparents as they all went in the rear door of Jessie's house.

"Your son cracks me up," Flint said, releasing the laugh he'd been so obviously holding in.

Jessie smiled at Flint's comment as she watched her youngest disappear inside.

The day had ended the way it had begun—at a picnic table. Only tonight it was the picnic table in Jessie's backyard where she, her four kids, her parents and Kelsey, Coop, Anthony and Flint had all shared the grilled chicken that Jeannie Hunt had prepared for dinner.

It was nearly nine o'clock now, however, and much the way the rest of the day and evening had gone, Kelsey had orchestrated things so that she and Coop took Anthony home at the same time that Jack and Jeannie Hunt were dispatched to put Ella, Braden, Bethany and Adam to bed, leaving Jessie and Flint sitting directly across from each other at the picnic table. Alone.

"They're all great kids," Flint added. "And every one of them looks like you. Especially Ella—she's a miniature version of you."

"I can see their father in each of the kids in small ways," Jessie answered Flint's observation, trying to hide her embarrassment at her sister's less-than-subtle manipulations to put them together. "She's also taller than I was at her age, and lanky, the way Pete was. And when she frowns—"

"Which she seems to do a lot," Flint remarked. "Especially when she sees me."

"I'm sorry about that. I know she's sort of treating you like the enemy. There was something about your catching me when I nearly fell off the drier yesterday..." Something that had also imprinted every tiny nuance on Jessie's brain to relive over and over again. "Well, whatever it was, Ella didn't like the look of it and you seem to be getting the full blame. I think she'll get over it in a day or two, but for now—"

"I'm not the guy who just kept you from falling, I'm the guy who got too up close and personal with her mom."

Up close and personal enough for Jessie to smell the clean, woodsy scent of his cologne. To see even more clearly the flecks of gold that illuminated his dark eyes. To have felt those steely shoulders in the grip of her own hands...

She swallowed hard, feeling as breathless as she had in the moment.

"Anyway, give her a day or two, and Ella will probably come around," Jessie finally managed to say when she'd dragged herself out of her split-second reverie.

Flint didn't respond to that, instead he went on with what they'd been talking about before. "And the twins, they seem like the spitting image of you, too. How do they look like their dad?"

"Their coloring is all Pete—the lighter hair and eyes. And Adam has Pete's smile and his turned-up nose."

Flint nodded, but his eyes were on her intently the whole time, as if he were gauging his words before he said, "Do you mind if I ask how he died?"

Not when it was asked so gently, so compassionately, so mindful of it being difficult for her to talk about.

She sighed. "It was an accident at a building site. A faulty crane, a dropped girder…" But she couldn't bring herself to go into the details, so she said, "We were both working for the same construction company— I ran the office, Pete was the electrical foreman, so he was in the field most of the time. Sometimes I had paperwork that would take me into the on-site office—that was always set up in a trailer that stayed on a big job—"

"Were you *there* when it happened?" Flint asked, his frown lines deep with horror on her behalf.

"I was," she said, her voice cracking even though it was barely above a whisper. "Thankfully I didn't see it, but I heard workman shouting, running, yelling for someone to call for an ambulance, which I did before I ever left the trailer or knew it was Pete I was calling for…"

"I'm so sorry," Flint said with heartfelt sympathy.

"He literally never knew what hit him, which was a blessing, I think. And I didn't have to see him—the owner of the company kept me away until they had Pete in the ambulance. I rode to the hospital holding his hand…"

Okay, she couldn't talk about that without breaking down, and she didn't want to break down. She'd done more than her share of crying. So she swallowed hard and said, "Things are pretty much a blur for me from there."

"That's probably a blessing, too, in this case."

"I know my folks were at the hospital by the time I got there. Kelsey wasn't living in Red Rock then, but she wasn't far away and she was at home with the kids by the time my folks brought me back. Telling them was the hardest thing I'd ever done."

"This was how long ago?"

"A little over two years."

"Were the kids even old enough to understand?"

"Adam was only a baby, so no. He doesn't even remember Pete except through pictures and stories I've told him. Braden and Bethany were two and a half, so they didn't really get it either. For a long time they just kept asking where Daddy was, when he was coming home, and we'd have to tell them all over again, try to help them understand—"

"But Ella, she was five, right?"

"Right. She knew exactly what was going on, poor thing." And that, too, brought the sting of tears to Jessie's eyes. But in two years she'd learned well how to hold them at bay. "Ella went back and forth between her own grief and putting up a strong front. Half the time she played parent—helping with the other kids, making an attempt to look after me…"

"Ross."

Jessie raised her eyebrows at Flint in question to his oldest brother's name.

"Ross did that in my family," Flint explained. "We all took care of each other, but it was Ross who led the way, who played parent."

Again Jessie wasn't sure exactly why that had been necessary, but not knowing the details, she assumed that it had something to do with his mother's overall less-than-stellar reputation.

"I suppose," Jessie said then, "that that's what's going on now, too— Ella is feeling protective. And maybe a little territorial."

"So we're being pushed *and* pulled," Flint said then with a knowing smile.

Jessie thought she knew what he meant, but she didn't want to assume too much so she merely repeated, "Pushed and pulled?"

"Ella wants to pull you away, to keep you to herself. But there's a lot of pushing going on with Kelsey, and now Coop and tonight your parents, too…"

"I know, I'm sorry," she apologized for the second time. "I was hoping maybe you hadn't noticed the not-so-veiled attempts at matchmaking."

Flint laughed again and Jessie wished she didn't like the sound of it as much as she did.

"You thought I hadn't noticed that we're being dispatched to paint rooms together, to go to the store together, to do *everything* they can possibly get us to do *together?* That seating arrangements always put us side by side—"

"And now this—" Jessie interjected, raising both hands in the air and glancing around "—getting everybody out of here so we're alone."

Flint grinned that great grin that drew such sexy lines on his handsome face. "Yep, I noticed. Impossible not to. It seems to be a conspiracy."

"But Kelsey is the mastermind."

"I think her intentions are good," Flint allowed.

"Oh, they are," Jessie was quick to confirm. "She just wants what she thinks is best for me." And it was a compliment to Flint that Kelsey thought he was it.

"The two of you are really close, aren't you?"

"She's not only my sister, she's also my best friend."

"And your folks, have you all always lived together?"

"No, they retired about the same time I lost Pete. They'd both worked for a small, independent paper company. They had planned to sell their house and do some traveling when the time came, but instead they moved in here with me to help get me through the loss and to lend a hand with the kids. They've been a godsend. Between them and Kelsey moving back to Red Rock eight months ago, I don't think I could have made it without them. But the matchmaking…all I can do is say I'm sorry."

Flint smiled again, not seeming perturbed by what her family—and his brother—were doing.

"It's not so bad," he said in a tone that seemed as if it might have held some innuendo, except that Jessie thought she was too out of practice with men to be sure. "I just don't know how that roof is going to get fixed if I don't get up there and give Coop a hand with it."

"I'll try again to reason with Kelsey," Jessie said as

Flint got to his feet, apparently ready to follow Kelsey and Cooper home.

Jessie stood, too, and without thinking about it, began to walk with Flint to the gate that connected her back-yard to Kelsey's.

"Maybe instead of that," he said along the way, "we should give them a little of what they want."

Jessie didn't have any idea what he was talking about that time. "Give them what they want?"

"Maybe we should pretend to go on a date together, come back and say we just didn't click. Maybe then they'd relax."

An instant wave of dejection—or maybe rejection— washed through her at the thought that Flint had decided they didn't click. That decision shouldn't have been jarring—after all, they didn't *need* to click beyond the friendly superficialities that were already in effect. There was no reason for anything more than that.

And she didn't *want* there to be anything more than that, Jessie reminded herself. This was strictly a distant, siblings-of-in-laws relationship.

And yet it was somehow demoralizing to hear that Flint didn't think they clicked…

Especially when she was so intensely aware of him in every way.

She hid her feelings behind what she hoped was noth-ing more than a curious expression and as they reached the gate, said, "A pretend date?"

Flint opened the gate, stood in the opening and turned to lean one shoulder against the six-foot-high side post so that he was facing her. "We'll go out alone, have dinner someplace innocuous— Not Red, where all eyes would be on us."

Red was the local restaurant owned by the Mendoza family, who were extremely close friends of the Fortunes. They even had family ties with them now that the Mendozas' son, Marcos, was engaged to Wendy Fortune—a member of the Atlanta branch of the Fortune family who had only recently come to Red Rock.

"All eyes would definitely be on us at Red," Jessie agreed.

"So we'll go somewhere else. How about that barbecue place outside of Austin that Coop and Kelsey were talking about tonight?"

"They seemed to like it."

"Then we'll come home, I'll say you're great but there just weren't any sparks. You can say I'm a big jerk if you want—"

Jessie laughed but didn't think it was wise to say that she already knew he wasn't a big jerk, so instead said, "I'll probably stick with the just-no-sparks thing, too."

"And then they'll all have to give it a rest."

Jessie considered the ruse. "I suppose you do have a point. If they think we gave it a try and it just didn't go anywhere, they'll have to accept it and back off."

"Not that I don't enjoy working with you and talking to you…" Flint added with a small but genuine smile that convinced her that he actually did. Even if they didn't *click*.

"But that roof is in bad shape," Flint went on, "and even with two of us it's going to be a big job. Unless you want to volunteer to work up there, then we can keep this going…"

"Mid-June Texas heat on a rooftop? I don't think so."

"We do a date, then?"

"I guess we could give it a try," Jessie agreed. "When?"

"Tomorrow night?"

"Okay."

"I'll tell Coop and Kelsey as soon as I get inside. Hopefully they'll figure if we're seeing each other socially tomorrow night, they don't need to push things in the day and Coop and I can get started on the roof."

"I'll keep my fingers crossed," Jessie promised.

"And then we'll have our fake date—at seven?"

"Sure."

"Ella's really going be mad at me after that, isn't she?" Flint asked.

"It's probably going to keep you blacklisted," she confirmed.

"I'll have to get you home early to convince everyone that the date is a flop—maybe that'll help."

And somehow the thought of making sure the date didn't last too long was also a bit of a downer.

But Jessie shooed that away. Flint was right, a short date was more likely to look like a failure. And that was what they were going for.

"Okay, then," Jessie said. "We have a pretend date tomorrow night at seven."

"For barbecue. And we'll just hope our plan works."

Jessie nodded her agreement, and in the process her gaze caught on his face once more. On his smoldering eyes. On lips that were so, so supple...

And why she should suddenly wonder if pretend dates ended with good-night kisses, she had no idea. But that was exactly what she was wondering. Along with what it might be like to be kissed by Flint.

But the moment she realized that was what was going through her mind, she jolted herself out of it, telling herself that of course there wouldn't be a good-night kiss. The whole point of the fake date was to convince their families that they *didn't* click.

"Guess I'll see you tomorrow for work first, though," Flint said then.

Which seemed like her cue to leave, so she said she would see him the next day and headed to her back door, pondering why she was looking forward to a date that was only for show.

Chapter Four

"Mama, you're so pretty!"

"Thank you, Braden," Jessie said to her four-year-old son.

She was putting on the finishing touches for her pretend date with Flint on Wednesday evening by trying to force earrings into pierced lobes that hadn't been used since Pete's funeral. It had somehow drawn the attention of all four kids, who were sitting or lying on her bed to watch.

"You look good as Miss Osterman," Bethany contributed, a compliment indeed because Miss Osterman had been the twins' twenty-two-year-old drop-dead gorgeous swimming instructor and Bethany had already announced that she wanted to look just like that when she grew up. *Who didn't?* had been what Kelsey and Jessie had answered with a laugh...

"You should stay home and eat with us," Ella contributed morosely, frowning at Jessie in the mirror that Jessie was facing, the mirror that reflected the kids behind her as well. "Gramma is making us macaroni and cheese with the squiggly noodles."

Oh, Ella, I'm sorry, Jessie thought. *But when this is over you'll be able to relax...*

"I wanna go," Adam lamented before Jessie could think of what to say to her oldest daughter. "I wanna eat with Fwint."

"No one's going but your mama," Jessie's mother said, apparently having overheard Adam as she'd approached the room because her response came at the same time she appeared in the doorway. "Tonight is for your mama and Flint—grown-ups only. Now let her get ready and come downstairs—supper's ready."

All four kids hopped up and Jessie turned from her dresser mirror to give Ella a hug as her oldest slipped off the bed.

"It'll be okay. You'll see," she whispered.

Ella didn't answer her, obviously not convinced.

Jessie's mother waved fluttering hands at her daughter. "Go on, get back to what you were doing. He'll be here soon and I have a surprise dessert for Ella—her favorite."

"Strawberry ice cream?" Ella said, barely enthusiastic.

"Strawberry ice cream with my special fresh strawberry sauce to put on top," Jeannie Hunt said as she shooed the kids out and pulled Jessie's bedroom door closed behind them all, leaving Jessie alone.

And torn between hating Ella's obvious displeasure

about her spending time with Flint Fortune and trying to figure out her own feelings.

She *shouldn't* feel *anything* about this date. Certainly not excitement. Or anticipation. Or eagerness. She definitely shouldn't have butterflies in her stomach. And there was no way she should have needed to change her clothes three times before settling on the khaki slacks and red camp shirt that was very—*very*—fitted. No way she should have deep-conditioned her hair so it would have extra wave and shine when she wore it down.

All for a date that wasn't real. A date that was nothing but subterfuge, a ploy to get her family to stop pushing her and Flint Fortune together.

Yet she *was* feeling excited and eager and there were butterflies in her stomach.

As if this were a real date.

And every bit of that also caused her guilt. Guilt for Ella's confusion and anger. And guilt over Pete, too...

She closed her eyes, took a deep breath and wished what she'd wished a million times since that day she'd lost her husband—that everything hadn't gotten so complicated, so difficult.

This wasn't the way it was supposed to be. She was supposed to be married to Pete, living her life and caring for the kids with him, looking forward to growing old together.

She wasn't supposed to be raising four kids alone. She wasn't supposed to be *dating*—for real or not.

And she wasn't supposed to be feeling any kind of attraction for a man who *wasn't* Pete...

That was just so weird. And unsettling. It made Jessie feel as if she were being disloyal to Pete.

"But it's not a real date," she told her reflection in

the mirror as she finally got one small hoop earring in and began to work on the second.

A fake date concocted to put an end to Kelsey's matchmaking. And once that was accomplished, Jessie reminded herself, she would again be free to put her energies into her kids. Which was what she was determined to do. Her family was her priority and nothing was going to change that.

And part of making them her priority meant that she was determined to be cautious about what—and who—she allowed into their lives.

Yes, Kelsey thought Flint was a decent guy and so far Jessie hadn't seen anything that said he wasn't. But he also wasn't from the best background—from what little Jessie knew.

Granted, she didn't know much, and she certainly didn't know any of the details, but she did know that Flint and Coop's mother had been married four times. That she'd had four children with three different fathers.

That had to have made an impression on Flint, and Jessie couldn't imagine that it had made a good one.

And because she knew, too, that Flint was divorced—though, again, without knowing any details—and he'd said himself that he was not to be tied down—she thought that it didn't speak well of his staying power and that that could potentially have come from his less-than-ideal background.

If there was one thing that Jessie was terrified of, it was feeling about someone the way she'd felt about Pete, and losing them. She just couldn't go through that again in any fashion—including divorce. She couldn't risk that kind of loss for herself and she wouldn't risk it for her kids.

If she ever took a chance on another man, it would have to be with someone she knew without a doubt would never choose to leave her. Someone who would stick around through thick and thin.

That someone wasn't likely to be a man who was accustomed to seeing his mother go in and out of marriages, who already had a divorce of his own under his belt and was clearly a commitment-phobe.

"Not that it matters. You don't click with him, remember?" she told her reflection sarcastically.

That tone of voice would have made Pete laugh. And suddenly, as had happened many times since his death, Jessie had such a strong sense of him that it made her wonder if his spirit was there with her.

Watching her get ready to go out with another man.

Pete had liked the earrings she was struggling to put on. Maybe she shouldn't wear them.

But somehow, even in her sense that Pete was with her, she didn't feel as if she needed to change her jewelry.

And that was when—out of the blue—another thought occurred to her that actually seemed to bear the mark of her late husband.

Pete had always been an optimistic, upbeat person. Even in the most dire situations she'd never known him not to find the good that could come of anything. And while having a fledgling attraction to another man wasn't a dire situation, it struck her at that moment that maybe the good to come out of it was that feeling even the slightest attraction to someone new, someone other than Pete, was a sign that she was becoming capable of moving on.

The idea gave her a twinge of guilt, too, but she knew taking that first step was an indication that she was healing. That healing meant regaining some emotional health and stamina and resiliency. It meant she was getting stronger. And strength—especially when she was raising four children—was exactly what she needed.

"So, wondering what the man looks like without his shirt on is okay?" she asked her reflection and the room in general.

When the question made her laugh a little, she decided it must be okay. That her secret appreciation of Flint's physical attributes were indeed a positive sign that she was coming out of her grief.

And since there was no danger of it going any further than that because he'd already let her know she didn't do anything for him, and because tonight's dinner was the beginning of the plan to get her sister and her sister's matchmaking minions to back off, Jessie decided she could look at the whole picture as a positive.

As just a reawakening, of sorts. Like the first blossoming of Texas bluebonnets in spring to mark the end of winter, feeling a hint of attraction to Flint Fortune marked the end of the emotional winter that had come over her with Pete's death.

It was nothing more than that.

So it was okay, she concluded. She could go on this pretend date with Flint, come home and get on with business as usual.

And if her heart skipped a beat when the doorbell rang and a moment later Braden called up the stairs, "Flint's here…"

It was just part of that secret attraction to the man that didn't really mean a thing.

And finally, firmly in that conviction, Jessie got the second earring in, took a last look at herself in the mirror, decided she was presentable enough and marched out of the room to meet her date.

The barbecue joint that Kelsey and Cooper had recommended was just outside Austin, so it didn't take Jessie and Flint long to get there.

Their conversation during the trip was merely about the best and worst barbecue they'd each had in the past, and about how to get to the place. But once they were seated at the round wooden table in the down-home roadside establishment that was part restaurant, part bar, part honky-tonk, Jessie knew it was time for a new vein of small talk.

And maybe coming up with some of that would keep her from admiring all that Flint could do to a plain pair of cowboy boots, a crisp white dress shirt and jeans that had made it impossible not to look at his rear end and his thighs every chance she got.

So she opted for satisfying one of the many pieces of curiosity she had about him and his family, and said, "Yesterday when William and Lily were at Kelsey's house someone mentioned the medallion Anthony wore when he was found. That keeps coming up—was it some kind of family heirloom or something?"

"You might say that. Not that we knew it until recently. There are four medallions—Ross, Coop, Frannie and I each had one, but we thought they were junk. We only learned recently from our mother—when we pushed her on the subject—that Uncle William gave them to her to give to us. Apparently he told her to make sure we knew that they were important keepsakes that had been in the family for generations."

"That isn't what she did?" Jessie asked.

"Not our mother," he said, somewhat disparagingly. "We had to piece it together ourselves. We think that the medallions were Uncle William's way of trying to help us feel part of the family, to give us a sense of connection. Which would have been really nice for us all to know because we always thought we were the black sheep. But with my mother, that wasn't how they were presented to us."

The drinks they'd ordered came and, with them, menus. But rather than looking at them yet, Jessie said, "How did she present them?"

"They were our Christmas gifts one year. We'd been left with a neighbor while Mom went off with her man-of-the-hour to Las Vegas the week before. She barely made it back for Christmas morning and our only presents were the medallions. I'm sure she'd forgotten all about getting us anything else and had taken out the medallions as a last-ditch effort to give us gifts. She told us they were from buried pirate treasure, which we believed at the time because we were all just little kids."

"Were you happy to get them?"

"At the time? They weren't what any of us had wanted, but sure. If my mother is good at anything it's spinning a tall tale. For weeks we used them to play pirate. They were our gold doubloons."

"But that didn't last?"

"You know how it is. Eventually the game got old, the medallions were stuck in drawers and as we grew up we all just figured they were worthless trinkets that she'd picked up in Vegas before she'd rushed home that year. We didn't think they had any value. Certainly not that they connected us to the Fortunes."

"But when Anthony showed up?"

"Ross saw the medallion and remembered them. Of course the baby wasn't Frannie's and Ross actually knew where his medallion was, so he wasn't ever in the running for Anthony's dad. But I couldn't find mine and neither could Coop—"

"Which initially meant that either of you could have been Anthony's father."

"That's how it seemed, yeah."

"And for you both there were multiple possibilities for women who could have come across your medallion and taken it?"

He had the good grace to smile sheepishly over his beer. "Anyone could have come across the medallions and taken them. But given that there was an almost-newborn with it strung around him, it was a good bet that a woman one of us had been involved with had taken it. About the same time the DNA results came back that cleared me, I found my medallion. I'm keeping it safer now. Coop got his back with Anthony, but when Uncle William saw it he seemed to recognize it and got agitated. He said it was his, so Coop let him keep it. Who knows, that might help get his memory to come back, too."

"I hope something does," Jessie said as the waitress returned to take their dinner order.

They both glanced quickly at the menu and ignored the recommendation of ribs, both choosing pulled pork sandwiches instead.

When the waitress had taken the menus and left, Flint settled back in his chair, leveled dark eyes on her and apparently took his turn at making small talk. "So tell me about yourself. Do you work?"

"Ha! You mean other than helping Kelsey get her house remodeled and decorated, wrangling four kids, doing a gazillion loads of laundry a week, cooking, cleaning, grocery shopping, driving car pool to a dozen different activities—"

He laughed. "I didn't mean to say you don't do plenty of work. I just meant—do you have a job on top of all that? You said you and your husband had worked at the same construction company."

"I couldn't go on working there after the accident," she confessed quietly. "There was life insurance on Pete and our mortgage was paid off with a death benefit rider on the house insurance, plus there was a settlement from the company, so I have some financial cushion. The first year after losing Pete it took everything I had just to get myself out of bed in the morning, just to take care of the kids—"

"I'm sure," Flint said sympathetically.

"But I do still have four kids to keep going, to hopefully send to college, so last year I started temping in the school district as a secretary. I liked working with the kids, the teachers and the principals were all great— there's sort of a community feel to working in a school that was really nice. The pay isn't wonderful, but I've applied for a full-time position next year because it would be a way to make a living without dipping into the nest egg too much, and it would give me hours and vacations similar to what the kids will have when they're all in school with Ella."

Their food arrived, but beyond thanking the waitress, Flint's attention remained on Jessie. "You've applied for a full-time job but you don't know if you got it?"

"Not yet—it's summer vacation. I was told not to expect to hear anything until July or even the first of August—just before the principals go back for the next year."

They tasted their sandwiches and decided Kelsey and Coop had been right about the food. Then, as they ate, Flint returned to the subject of her working.

"Will you put Braden, Bethany and Adam in day care until they start?"

Jessie couldn't imagine that he was actually interested in any of this, but his eyes only left her to glance at his food. They never strayed to even the curviest of the waitresses, and he seemed completely intent on Jessie, as well as genuinely listening to what she said. It was nice.

So, hoping she wasn't boring him to tears, she answered his question.

"Braden and Bethany are in preschool this year—I found one that really focuses on preparation for kindergarten and it runs four mornings a week. So the twins will be gone a lot. Adam is starting preschool this year, but his will be more playtime and it's only two afternoons. But my folks have promised to stay as long as I need them and they can get everybody where they have to be while I work, and babysit when the kids are home."

Despite Flint's interest—or at least the appearance of it—Jessie felt as if she'd talked too much about herself, so she said, "What about you? Have you always done what you're doing now—selling Western arts and crafts?"

He laughed. "Not by a long shot," he said before going on to regale her with tales of other sales jobs as well as a laundry list of different things he'd tried his hand at, beginning with lawn mowing jobs when he was ten.

"Wow, you really are a jack-of-all-trades," Jessie marveled.

"My résumé says I'm diverse," he joked. "But I've been doing what I'm doing now for the last eight years and I'm sticking with it."

They'd finished eating by the time he'd completed the list of his various occupations and Jessie wasn't sure if it was the relaxed atmosphere they were in or Flint's winning charm that had somehow put her at ease. But the jitters she'd been in the grip of earlier were gone and she realized she was actually enjoying herself. Enjoying talking and listening to him.

But their meal was over and she expected him to suggest they put phase two into play—ending the evening early to make it more convincing that they hadn't *clicked*.

Instead, the band that provided the live music promised on the sign outside took the stage at the other end of the place, gave a rebel-rousing yell and announced that it was time for some line dancing. With a glimmer in his eye, Flint raised a challenging brow at her. "What do you say?"

Jessie loved to dance and hadn't done it in longer than she could remember.

"Really?" she asked.

"I don't know why not."

Jessie knew there must be some reasons why not, but at that moment she couldn't think of any. She also couldn't keep from smiling and taking him up on the dance—which *was* only a line dance, she told herself. Line dancing was innocent enough—it wasn't as if she'd be in Flint's arms or anything.

So with Flint helping her ease her chair away from their table, she stood and together they went with many of the other customers to the wooden dance floor.

To aid her recollection, Jessie kept a close eye on every move Flint made beside her, following his lead until she no longer needed to. Or maybe a little longer than she needed to just so she could keep glancing over at him because watching him dance was something to see.

He had a kind of loose-limbed cowboy grace and a casual confidence that echoed in every step, every gesture. He was light on his big, booted feet. Those long legs of his were flexible and powerful at once. His broad shoulders dipped with such a sexy sway that it made Jessie's mouth go dry. And when he hooked his thumbs into his front pockets and drew her eyes to his hips… It wasn't the dancing that took her breath away.

It didn't end up being an early evening after all. Before Jessie knew so much time had passed, it was last call and the place was closing. And even then Flint persuaded her to stay for the final dance before they left with everyone else and returned to Flint's rental car.

"Mothers are not supposed to close bars," she jokingly chastised as Flint opened the passenger door for her.

"That's not a theory *my* mother ever subscribed to," he answered wryly.

Shutting the door, he went around to get behind the wheel, and once they were on the road to home he said, "So if closing bars isn't how you have fun, what is?"

Jessie laughed, feeling tired, a little giddy and so, so much more relaxed than she had been even before all the dancing. "What do I do for fun...?" she reiterated. "I get away to the studio whenever I can."

"What studio? Explain."

"Pete turned the garage out back into a one-room apartment about five years ago. We rented it, but that turned out to be more hassle than it was worth and attracted some people we were worried about having around the kids. So I took it over as a sort of studio. Or maybe I should say a workshop."

"To sort of do what kind of work? Art?"

Jessie made a face because it seemed like putting on airs to say what she did was art. "It's more just a hobby I have. I make stone sculptures. But really it's just a chance for me to get out into the woods with the kids— hike a little, enjoy the scenery and collect stones. Then I use the stones to put together these sculptures—my versions of rock formations, I guess."

"Is that where you're going off to tomorrow? Coop said we'd be working in the morning, but that in the afternoon he and Kelsey have to take Anthony in for a well-baby checkup, and that you had other plans."

"That's exactly where I'll be. We make a whole outing of it—I bring hot dogs, we build a fire, make s'mores for dessert—" And then maybe because she was feeling slightly giddy, without considering the wisdom in it, she heard herself say, "Would you like to come with us?"

Flint took his eyes off the road to glance at her. To

smile. To surprise her by saying, "I think I would. I toast a mean marshmallow."

Jessie laughed. "Then you'll fit right in."

"Will I? Or will it ruin Ella's time if I come?"

He won points for thinking of her daughter and Jessie considered the effect it might have on Ella to include Flint in this family outing. But in the end she said, "Ella probably won't be thrilled, but it also might give her the chance to give *you* a chance. She's made a snap judgment of you and it might be good for her to get to know you, to see you in a different light."

Flint smiled at her again. "Assuming that when she gets to know me she doesn't still hate me."

The more Jessie had come to know him tonight, the more she liked him. Liked just how pleasant and easy to talk to he was, how easy it was to be with him—much as she wished that wasn't the case. But because it was, she couldn't imagine that eventually Ella wouldn't warm to him, too, and come to let go of her unfounded resentment of the man who would soon be like an uncle to her.

"I have faith in you," Jessie informed him in a way that goaded him a little and made him chuckle a throaty chuckle that she found all too sexy.

They'd arrived home by then, though, and Flint parked at the curb in front of Kelsey's house.

Jessie didn't wait for him to come around to her door. She met him at the front fender and wondered if they would merely say good-night there and go to their respective houses—which would aid the cause of convincing everyone that this had not been a successful date.

But Flint motioned in the direction of her house and walked her to her door.

It was so late that there was no question about asking him in, although the thought did flit through her mind—shocking her a bit.

But standing in the glow of porch light at her door, she merely faced him.

Before she had said the good-night she intended to say, however, she found Flint looking into her eyes, smiling a warm, intimate smile that somehow stalled the farewell.

"I know we're not supposed to let anybody else in on this," he whispered, "but I had a great time."

"Me, too," Jessie whispered back guilelessly, following it with a nod in the direction of Kelsey's house. "But the roof needs fixing and we have to get everyone to leave us alone," she reminded.

"Right..." he said, not sounding fully on board with that. "So I guess we say..."

"We didn't click," she repeated with a hint of facetiousness to that last word.

"We didn't click," Flint echoed as if nothing could be further from the truth. "Except that I'm going rock hunting with you tomorrow."

"Oh, that's right," Jessie said, making a face when she realized that contradicted the goal of tonight's outing.

"We could say," Flint suggested, "that I didn't know what I was going to do with myself while Coop and Kelsey were gone to the pediatrician and you took pity on me, invited me to go along—just as friends—to give me something to do."

"Just as friends—we'll have to really push that," Jessie said. "Let's try it."

He grinned. "What's the worst that can happen? They'll all still keep putting us together and we'll just have to have another pretend date to confirm that we don't click."

Jessie laughed. "Or maybe we could just let them all see that we can be friends and only friends, and leave it at that."

"Friends..." he repeated without much fondness for that word. But then he seemed to accept it, and said, "As long as I still get to go rock hunting."

"Because it's long been a dream of yours," she teased.

"It has," he insisted, playing along.

But it was the end of the evening and Jessie knew they should be saying good-night and parting ways.

Yet she still went on standing where she was, looking up into Flint's handsome face, letting his eyes delve into hers, trying not to think about the good-night kiss that seemed as if it should come at the conclusion of the kind of evening they'd just shared.

Then Flint grasped her shoulders, pulled her slightly forward, leaned toward her...

And kissed her forehead.

Sure, he stayed there a moment longer than he should have—long enough for her to feel the warmth of his breath in her hair—but only a moment before he pulled back, let go of her and said, "See you tomorrow."

"See you tomorrow," she parroted in barely more than another whisper, remembering only belatedly to actually open her front door and go into the house as he headed across the yards to her sister's place.

And although she was telling herself as she went in that not even the kiss on the forehead should have happened, it didn't change the fact that she was secretly wishing for more.

And feeling guilty for that wish.

More guilty still for the craving to feel Flint Fortune's lips on hers.

Chapter Five

"We're supposed to hoist shingles onto the roof before breakfast?" Flint said as he and Coop went out to the garage early Thursday morning at the instruction of Kelsey.

"We're supposed to hoist shingles onto the roof while Kelsey makes breakfast," Coop qualified as he got the wheelbarrow off the garage wall and they began to load packs of shingles into it. "But you know the real reason—she can't wait for me to find out how your date with Jessie was last night."

After only four hours of sleep Flint was not at the top of his game. But even so the mere mention of that date made him want to smile.

He didn't. He worked not to because he had some convincing to do and he knew the time had come. But it took effort to instead make the most pained face he could muster and lie through his teeth.

"The date was not good," he complained.

"But Kelsey said she got up with Anthony at one this morning and you were still out—how does a bad date go on past one in the morning?"

"Yeah, well, I had to make it look good, didn't I? Jessie is Kelsey's sister after all."

"But you had a lousy time?" Cooper asked, sounding confused.

"There's just nothing there, Coop. You know how it is."

"With Jessie? There's nothing there with Jessie?"

"Who else are we talking about?" Flint said, taking the offensive because his brother seemed completely confounded by the notion that there wasn't any attraction between Flint and Jessie.

"But every time the two of you are together—"

"Right. Again, making it look good," Flint insisted as he plopped another bundle of shingles into the wheelbarrow. "I'm not saying that she isn't nice and pretty and what have you. I'm just saying that she doesn't do anything for me. And I don't do anything for her. We don't…click."

Liar.

"Is it the kids?" Coop asked, apparently unable to believe that it was as simple as Flint was making it out to be.

"Well, come on, *four* kids, Coop," Flint said. "That's—"

"I know, it's a lot. And you and I and Frannie and Ross, with our background…there's nothing to recommend family life in that. I mean, I love my son and I wouldn't trade him for anything, but coming to grips with the fact that I *have* a son? That was something. If it wasn't for Kelsey I'd have been lost." Coop shook his head. "So I get it. Taking on someone else's four kids would be huge to sign on for, no matter how great Jessie is."

And Jessie *was* great, Flint thought. Beautiful and fun and smart and sweet—and *wow* could she move on a dance floor when she got into it!

But he liked to keep things light and breezy with women, and light and breezy with a woman with four kids just wasn't going to happen.

Or if it *did* happen, to him it would mean that the woman was the kind of mother his own mother had been. And carelessly letting a man come between her and her kids was something he could never respect.

"It's just better if Jessie and I are nothing but friends," Flint said then, even though he'd really chafed at *that* word when Jessie had said it last night. Because for a moment he'd lost sight of everything but the beauty standing in front of him—the woman he'd had a terrific time with, the woman he'd been wanting so badly to kiss the desire had been eating him alive. And there she was, saying they needed to just be *friends*. The ultimate rejection.

Not that he'd been feeling rejected when she'd said it with that little smile that put the damned cutest dimple just above the left corner of her mouth…

"So you're going to the woods with her and the kids today as friends?" Coop asked then.

Just before Flint had come out to the garage with his brother he'd told Kelsey not to expect him for dinner tonight and why.

Flint shrugged. "Jessie is nice and so are her kids. It's not as if I don't like them all."

"You just don't want to get into anything serious."

"Exactly," Flint answered honestly. "And if you can get Kelsey to see that it's nothing against her sister, but that there just can't be more to it than Jessie and I knowing each other, maybe hanging out a little, being friendly, I'd really appreciate it."

"I'll do what I can," Coop promised. "But I'll leave the kids out of it. Kelsey has been so good about taking on me *and* Anthony, I'm pretty sure she wouldn't think too kindly of somebody not wanting to be daddy to her nieces and nephews. I'll just tell her the 'no chemistry between you' thing."

"Whatever it takes to keep the peace and still get Kelsey to give up the matchmaking so we can replace the shingles."

"I'm all for that!" Coop said as he grasped the wheelbarrow's handles and rolled it out of the garage with Flint following behind, carrying one more bundle on his shoulder.

But even as he did, Flint was thinking *no chemistry, no clicking—it would be so much easier if any of that was actually true.*

But despite the fact that it wasn't—that there was so much chemistry and "clicking" for him when it came to Jessie that being nothing but friends with her was going to be one of the toughest things he'd ever done—he knew he had to do it.

It would be bad enough for him, for Jessie, if they got involved and it ran the same course he'd watched his mother run with all the men in her life—the same course his own marriage had taken. Dragging her four kids along for the ride would only make it worse.

So, light and breezy it is, he told himself.

And he was determined to make it stick.

Even if he had lain awake for too long last night after leaving Jessie at her door, remembering the sweet smell of her hair and the softness of her skin under his lips when he'd kissed her forehead.

And remembering, too, just how much he'd wanted to pull her into his arms, hold her against him and kiss her lips instead.

The situation just wasn't right for any of them. Jessie *was* a mother of four and he was not in any way, shape or form a family man.

And that was all there was to it.

"Okay, pick one again!"

"No, Braden," Jessie told her son. "No more 'pick which hand the rock is in.' It's time to go."

"You can see it anyway," Bethany said. "You gotta use a smaller rock, Braden."

"The fire is out, everything is packed up—now all of you get in the van," Jessie commanded for the third time.

Darkness was falling. They'd had a full afternoon of rock hunting, the cookout had filled everyone's belly with hot dogs and beans and various other side dishes that Jessie had brought in plastic containers, and they'd roasted an entire bag of marshmallows to squish between graham crackers and chocolate bars.

As a rule on these jaunts, Jessie left for home long before darkness fell. Because Flint was with them, that had added an entirely different element to the occasion, so she'd let things go on longer than usual. But now they really did need to leave.

Ella alone had taken Jessie's urgings for that seriously. The seven-year-old was already in her seat in the van. Clearly only too willing to put an end to this, she'd gone the first time Jessie had announced that they needed to go home. Now Ella was waiting with the disapproving scowl that she'd managed to maintain despite every attempt to get her to enjoy herself. But the twins and Adam were still fluttering around Flint, ignoring his futile attempts to get them to listen to their mother.

They'd taken teaching Flint about rock collecting very seriously and tutored him during that portion of the outing. But since returning to the campsite for dinner Flint had become their audience for clumsy attempts to fool him with silly four-year-old tricks, bad jokes and—in the case of Adam—just plain showing off and periodically climbing onto Flint's broad back and wrapping tiny arms around his thick neck in demands for piggyback rides.

Which was how Flint finally got Adam to the van—offering a piggyback ride that got the three-year-old onto his back, legs wrapped around his middle, Adam's arms choking the life out of Flint's neck, at the same time that Flint hauled Bethany under one arm, and Braden under the other, while walking like a stiff-limbed robot and making monster noises that delighted them all.

But at least he finally got them to the van. One by one he deposited each giggling child inside, laughing as they went to their respective seats to be securely belted in by Jessie.

Once that was accomplished, she said, "Ella won the

coin toss, so she gets to choose the movie for the ride home. What's it going to be, El?"

"Beauty and the Beast," Ella said with a glare at Flint that was embarrassingly obvious.

But Jessie merely said, *"Beauty and the Beast it is."*

Then she flipped down the small screen that came out of the van's ceiling to face the rear seats, put the DVD into the player and turned it on.

With all of the kids' eyes on that, she got out of the van's side door, slid it closed and faced Flint who was still standing nearby, watching.

"Sorry about Ella," she whispered.

"It's okay," he assured. Then, as if to prove her daughter's hostility was nothing to worry about, he dropped the subject and nodded toward the front of the silver van. "Are you sure you don't want me to drive home—I don't mind."

"No, I'm fine. You're probably more worn out than I am—the kids really ran you ragged."

"I'm fine, too," he said, but she still insisted on driving.

As Flint got into the passenger seat, Jessie went around and climbed behind the wheel. By the time she'd done that Flint was angled in her direction, his arm stretched across the back of the driver's seat.

It was slightly unnerving to have him looking at her as she turned the key in the ignition and put the van into gear, but it was also nice to have his undivided attention.

She had to back out onto the nearby road that led to the highway, and as she did Flint looked out the rear window, too, apparently catching sight of the kids in the process.

"Wow, they're already asleep," he marveled.

Jessie laughed. "It always happens—the woods, the hiking, the rock collecting and then full tummies—they can't stay awake for the trip home."

"Shall I turn off the movie?"

"No, that'll wake them up. Just let it play," she advised as she turned onto the highway from the side road. Then, with a sideways glance at Flint, she said, "Sooo... Did you just hate all of this today and tonight?"

He looked surprised by the question. "Are you kidding? I had a fantastic time!"

"Even with all of Ella's dirty looks and thinking you should have to eat the marshmallow that fell in the dirt?"

Flint laughed. "Yeah, I'm sorry that Ella still thinks I'm an evil interloper who only deserves dirt-laced marshmallows. And I know I shouldn't be, but I'm also a little sorry that I didn't get to spend much time with you."

Despite the fact that he said the words as if he probably shouldn't, they still sent a warm flush across Jessie's face that she hoped he couldn't see in the waning light. She also didn't want to acknowledge the impact such a small thing could have on her, so she made a joke of it. "You did miss out on going with me on some really fun trips to the bathrooms with one kid or another."

Flint smiled as if he knew what she was doing, but he didn't push it. Instead he said, "I just played with the kids, like one of the kids. You did end up doing most of the work—seems unfair."

"You were the marshmallow toaster—that helped.

And you were right, you do toast a mean marshmallow," she teased him.

"Yeah, but that was just fun, too. And I suppose that made Ella's point—I *did* drop the marshmallow in the dirt, so it would have served me right to have to eat it."

"A seven-year-old's reasoning."

"And *Beauty and the Beast?*" he said with a grin. "I think there might be a message in that. And it isn't that I'm the beauty."

"I really am sorry," Jessie apologized again, unable not to laugh at her daughter's barely veiled jibe.

"I think I can take a little heat from a seven-year-old. And I'm actually glad to see that you aren't trying to force her to act like she likes me—that's what *my* mother would have done. It just made us hate whatever guy she was ramming down our throats even more."

Jessie flinched. "Does it seem like I'm ramming you down their throats?"

"No!" he was quick to answer. "My mother would refer to some perfect stranger as Uncle So-and-So and expect us to act like they really were family. She'd fall all over them while we were there to see it. She liked to pretend that every man she ran through her life and ours was the be-all-and-end-all of existence, and God help us if we didn't keep up the charade. I don't think even Ella would say you did anything like that."

His mother was one of the people in his life Jessie was curious about, and now that he'd opened that door, she felt more invited to explore what was behind it. So she said, "I don't know much about your mom, but Kelsey did say that you and Cooper are half brothers, not full brothers. And I know your mom was married more than once…"

"Four times," Flint said as if it were no secret and he didn't have a problem with her asking. "There were no kids with Husband Number One. Ross and Cooper had the same dad—Husband Number Two. I came from Husband Number Three—Parker Anderson. And Frannie's dad was Number Four—Elliot Jones. He was the best of the lot, but he died. The other three were divorces."

"Your father wasn't the best of the lot?"

Flint shrugged fatalistically. "He's kind of a fly-by-night, from what little I know about him."

"You don't know him?"

"Sure, I know him. Technically. But I was too young to remember him being around, so I've only known him through sporadic visits now and then, when he decides to pop in. It isn't as if we have any kind of relationship—something I always envied of friends who had dads who were actually there for them."

He added that last part with a more solemn tone to his voice and Jessie knew that even though he didn't have a problem telling her the facts about his parents, when he mentioned his own feelings of jealousy, it struck home for him.

It also struck home for her, and she suddenly confessed one of her greatest fears and something she tried not to think might happen.

"I worry that my kids will feel that way without Pete—envious of kids who have fathers around. I always hope that having my dad in their lives, and now Coop, too, will help fill the void a little."

Flint must have realized how much of a worry this was to her because his tone softened. "It should help.

I know it would have helped us to have had a better, closer relationship with the Fortune men—Ryan before he died, Uncle William…"

"None of the other men your mother brought into your life fit the bill?"

"A few tried and sometimes for a while it would be nice, but… I don't mean to make my mother sound malicious or anything, she's just flighty and not really what you could call mature, even at seventy-two, and certainly not maternal in any way. So even the good guys, the ones she married, the ones we liked, were still in and out. And then Mom would be on to the search for the Man of Her Dreams, who she was sure she was going to find any day. To *this* day—although I imagine her fantasy of what he'll provide has changed."

"What he'll provide?"

Flint chuckled mirthlessly. "She was always telling us that the right man would buy us a big house with a yard for us to play in, and a swimming pool and a wooden playground set—like your dad is building for your kids now."

There was sadness to those words and Jessie's heart ached for the young Flint and his brothers and sister, for the dreams his mother had spun for them, for his early disappointments.

"But it never happened?" Jessie asked to be sure, hoping she might be wrong.

"Never happened," he confirmed. "Instead there was just a string of men, a string of different places we moved to to find a new man, different schools, and always, always some sort of chaos and drama that revolved around Cindy Fortune that even her own kids had to accommodate."

"And she never considered bringing you all back to Red Rock to live? Where you could have had extended family and genuine father figures?"

He smiled at her. "That's the kind of thinking you do—what might be good for your kids. I admire that. Watching you with them today, the last few days? They don't know how good they have it to have a mom like you. But I'm definitely impressed."

Which made Jessie feel very self-conscious. Even more so than having had his eyes on her throughout this whole drive.

"But your mom…" she said to encourage him to go on to what he'd seemed to be about to say.

"For my mom, factoring in what might be good for her kids when she made her own decisions wasn't something she could do. Maybe it was the way she was raised or who knows what, but to her, kids were like pets or like the couch and the coffee table—she had her life to live and we were just part of the background."

"And none of you ever suggested to her that you might be better off here?"

"Nah. We were here so seldom that we never felt like real Fortunes, even if we did carry the name."

"What about now?" Jessie asked as something else occurred to her. "Now that you know the truth about the medallions, now that you know the rest of your family *didn't* think of you all as the black sheep, do you feel more a part of things? Because you and Cooper both seem to be fitting in pretty well with them all, from what I've seen…"

"Actually," he said in a much lighter tone, "since having this new perspective on things, yeah, it has been different for me here. I feel like I'm reconnecting with the family. I'm beginning to see that no one has really held my mother's sins against any of us, that that was more in our own heads. And it's nice."

They arrived home at that moment and when Jessie pulled into her driveway her parents came out the front door. Apparently they'd been watching for her.

"Wow, curbside service," Flint observed with a laugh.

From the rearview mirror, Jessie saw that turning off the car engine was enough to wake Ella. When her eldest realized they were home, Ella roused Bethany and Braden.

Braden instantly sat up straight and said, "I don't want to go to sleep! I don't want those bad dreams!"

"It's okay, Braden," Jessie soothed as she and Flint unfastened their own seat belts simultaneously. "Braden has been having really bad nightmares," she explained. "I guess he doesn't realize he was already asleep and *not* having them."

"Poor guy," Flint sympathized as they got out of the vehicle just as Jack and Jeannie Hunt reached the van and Jessie climbed into the back portion to get to the kids.

Ella had released her own seat belt by then and was helping Braden and Bethany with theirs. Jessie's father collected Adam. Only when his grandfather had lifted him out of his car seat did the boy wake up.

Even still half-asleep, he searched for sight of Flint and said, "Can you come for game night?"

Flint laughed. "They're all a little punchy," he whispered to Jessie as she climbed from the van and turned to help Ella, while Flint offered Braden and Bethany a steadying hand to jump down.

"Game night," Bethany managed to explain in the process, as if Flint required enlightenment. "Tomorrow night is game night."

"Yeah. Can Fwint come?" Adam repeated.

"We'll talk about it tomorrow," Jessie said. "For now you all just need to get to bed."

"We'll do that," Jeannie Hunt assured, wasting no time heading all the kids toward the house.

"I'll be in in a minute to say good-night," Jessie called after them as she slid the van's side door closed again.

"Let me help you unload," Flint offered as she tugged her T-shirt down to the waistband of her jeans to adjust things that had gone awry in the transfer of children.

"I'll just leave everything for the morning," she said. "Between my parents, the kids and me, we'll do it all in one trip."

"You're sure?"

"Positive," she confirmed.

Flint didn't just say good-night then, though, and go next door. Instead he stood beside the van, looking at her in the distant glow coming from the porch light, making her wonder suddenly—and for no reason that made any sense—if her ponytail was still neat and if the blush and mascara she'd applied just before leaving today had stayed on.

"I really did have a great time," he said, stretching a long arm to the roof of the van and leaning slightly in that direction. Which also brought him somewhat closer to Jessie.

Since he'd joined them this afternoon she'd been secretly admiring the way he looked in his cowboy boots, jeans and a lightweight V-necked sweater that exposed a deep hollow in his throat below his Adam's apple. Now that sexy hollow caught her gaze for a moment before she forced herself to look up again, wondering why the sight of just a hint of beard shadowing that holy-hell-handsome face should add to his allure.

Then she reminded herself that he'd said he'd had a good time and was probably waiting for a response. "I'm glad," she answered, hoping it wasn't noticeably slow in coming.

"Your kids really are lucky to have a mom like you," he added, harking back to what they'd been talking about on the drive home.

Jessie laughed slightly. "I think *I'm* lucky to have *them*."

"Yeah, it shows."

She could tell that he was again recalling his mother's shortcomings and she felt bad for him, for the childhood he'd had. But she didn't know what to say about that, so instead she said, "I don't know if it matters to you, but you're pretty good with kids yourself—with Anthony and with my kids."

It was his turn to laugh. "I don't really do much."

"Still, you're not standoffish at all, the way a lot of people who don't have kids of their own are. I appreciate that you're patient with them, especially with Ella being kind of nasty and Adam wanting to crawl all over you. And I saw you pointing out the best rocks, so the kids could be the ones to pick them up and take the credit—you put them and their little egos ahead of yourself to make sure they had a good time and got to be proud of themselves—"

He laughed again. "Yep, that's me," he demurred, "not the glory seeker when it comes to rock hunting."

She hadn't seen anything about him that would have

caused her to think of him as a glory seeker and she liked that humility in him, too. But she didn't say it because she thought she'd already embarrassed him a little by praising the way he was with the kids.

"I'm just glad you had a good time. Or, if you're only saying you did to be polite, I hope it wasn't too awful."

Rather than answer that immediately, he merely studied her with a small, thoughtful smile that might have made her uncomfortable coming from someone else. But from Flint that scrutiny, that smile, somehow just wrapped around her like a warm blanket.

Then he said, "So far, I haven't spent five minutes with you that were awful, and I can't imagine that that's even possible. What *was* kind of lousy—and also one of the toughest lies I've ever told—was telling my brother this morning that we didn't hit it off."

Oh.

Jessie was really at a loss for what to say to *that*. Especially because hearing it from him had set something inside her jumping for joy. And trying to contain it only complicated her attempts to come up with a verbal response.

Then she heard herself say in a much more flirtatious tone than she'd intended, "Have you told a lot of lies in your lifetime?"

His smile went crooked. "Not too many whoppers like that one, no."

She could only stand there grinning up at him, lost in dark eyes that were trained on her with such intensity that she couldn't seem to tear her own eyes away.

Then, suddenly, without even knowing how she knew it, she knew he was going to kiss her.

And just as certainly, she knew he shouldn't, that she shouldn't let him. And that she could keep it from happening if she just took a step backward, away from the van and him, if she stopped answering his stare with one of her own, if she dropped her chin, if she just said good-night and went into the house…

But she didn't do any of that.

In fact, she tipped her chin upward just a bit, even as she told herself not to. Even as she thought about how she'd only ever kissed two people besides Pete— one boy in junior high, one in high school—and no one since him. Even as she worried that she might not remember how, or be really bad at it, or at least really, really rusty…

You shouldn't, Jess…

But when Flint began to lean toward her, she held her ground with her chin already up.

And when his mouth first met hers she wasn't thinking about the how-to's—she didn't need to. It felt perfectly natural to answer the sweet warmth of his lips as they brushed hers so lightly it was as if they almost weren't there at all.

And then to wish it wasn't over so quickly—that she didn't get to do even more.

But it was over so, so quickly. Too quickly for her to have closed her eyes. Almost too quickly to have happened at all, except that she could still feel his mouth on hers even after he'd pulled away and was just smiling down at her once more.

"Game night, huh?" he said, his voice deeper, more gravelly than it had been before.

"Once a week we have game night," she confirmed, recalling that Adam had essentially extended an invitation. "Is that something you'd be interested in?" she asked with some disbelief.

His smile stretched mischievously. "I'd hate to disappoint Adam. But then there's Ella," Flint pointed out.

"We can have Kelsey and Coop and Anthony come, too, and make it a whole-family game night this week. Ella likes it when we do that."

"Then everybody would be happy?"

Jessie knew she was suddenly looking forward to game night more than she had on other weeks. But she only said, "It would make Ella happ*ier* anyway."

"And you?"

He wanted to know if she wanted to see him again. It made Jessie smile. "It would be nice if you came," she confessed quietly, as if someone other than Flint might hear her.

"So tomorrow night we play games," he joked.

I think we might be playing one right now, she thought. But she said, "And eat hoagie sandwiches and chips and my mom's homemade chocolate cookies, and sit around on the living room floor to do it all—I have to warn you that it isn't fancy."

He was still holding her gaze and his smile seemed more intimate than it had been. "I don't care," he assured her, as if letting her know that what they did together didn't matter.

And again what washed through Jessie had no business washing through her.

Then he bobbed forward and kissed her again—so quickly this time that she didn't see it coming, didn't respond and—worst of all—barely got to enjoy it, before he said, "Tomorrow working on the house, tomorrow night for game night. I'll see you then."

Jessie nodded and they finally said good-night—without any more kissing—and went in opposite directions.

But as she stepped over the threshold, she couldn't keep herself from looking in the direction of her sister's house to catch a last glimpse of Flint.

Who stood with a booted foot on the bottom step of Kelsey's front porch, his hand on the railing, watching her, maybe waiting to make sure she got safely inside.

And without thinking that it might be juvenile or adolescent or silly, Jessie found herself waving to him, feeling a thrill at the sight of him raising a single, big hand in the air to return it.

Just before she went into her house, thinking that if this wasn't "clicking," she didn't know what was.

Chapter Six

"Mama, you overseeped! Gramma says you bey'er ge' up."

Jessie almost never overslept. But Adam was right—when she opened her eyes on Friday morning at the sound of her youngest's voice coming from her doorway and looked at the clock, she realized that that was exactly what she'd done.

It was Flint's fault. She hadn't been able to fall asleep after he'd kissed her the night before. Because even if that kiss hadn't been earth-shattering, it had still been enough to get Jessie's long-slumbering motor running just a little bit.

And she'd gone to bed with that excitement jockeying for position with guilt at the thought that she'd kissed another man and been unfaithful to Pete—because that was how it had felt.

Then somehow the guilt had faded and she'd found herself fantasizing about kissing Flint again, imagining kisses that weren't as innocent as that one had been. Imagining kisses that were longer, deeper, more passionate. Imagining more than kisses...

And then another wave of guilt had come on the heels of *that*.

It had been a long time before she'd been able to sleep.

But then she'd dreamed that Pete was okay with her kissing Flint...

She remembered it suddenly—a split second before Adam bounded onto her bed, and Ella, Braden and Bethany all came charging into her room.

"Good morning," she said, greeting the four reasons why—even if she had dreamed that Pete was okay with her kissing Flint—it still wasn't so okay.

"Gramma wants to know are you sick?" Ella asked.

Jessie sat up against her headboard. "No, I just slept through my alarm."

"She's not sick, Gramma," Ella shouted in her loudest voice.

Braden piped up, "I told her you wasn't—"

"Weren't," Jessie corrected his grammar.

"I told her you *weren't* sick when you came in to make me wake up from the bad dream last night."

"Is that why you're so tired?" Ella asked. "'Cuz Braden woke you up with the nightmares again?"

Jessie had been wide awake when that had happened, and long after she'd gotten Braden back to sleep and returned to her own bed. And to her thoughts of Flint.

But it was easier to let them all think she was tired

from being up with Braden than to tell them the truth, so she mussed up Braden's hair and said, "I'm sorry you had bad dreams again last night."

"Me, too!" Braden lamented.

"Gramma says Aunt Kelsey and Coop and Anthony and Flint are gonna come for game night tonight," Bethany said then. "Are they?"

"I don't know. I talked to Gramma about it before we went to bed last night. Did she talk to Aunt Kelsey?"

"They're coming," Ella said fatalistically.

"Fwint's comin'!" Adam confirmed, causing his oldest sister to glare at him.

"And so are Aunt Kelsey and Coop and Anthony, right?" Jessie said to defuse Ella's disapproval.

"Yeah, they're coming, too," Ella conceded as if that was the only redeeming factor.

"With Fwint!" Adam just couldn't get past that.

"I like Flint," Braden said, clearly siding with Adam against Ella.

"He's funny and nice," Bethany chimed in, too.

Although Jessie knew this was becoming the kind of three-against-one struggle her kids often engaged in, their sentiments made Jessie recall the conversation she'd had with Flint on the drive home from rock hunting the previous evening. And that caused her decision to act on something that had troubled her along with thoughts of Flint kissing her.

"I think we should talk about Flint," she said then, not wanting her kids to feel any of what he'd felt as a child when his mother had brought men into their family; and also wanting to make sure that any blossoming attachments her own kids might have to him were tempered with some realities.

"You all know that Flint is Coop's brother and that he's only visiting Aunt Kelsey and Coop, right? He doesn't live in Red Rock—"

"Where *does* he live?" Braden asked.

"In Denver, Colorado. And that's where he'll go back to when his visit is over."

"I wan' him to stay here," Adam decreed.

"But he won't be staying here," Jessie said gently but firmly. "He's only a visitor and I want you all to remember that. When his visit is over, he'll go back to his own home and we might not ever see him again."

Which was something she needed to keep in mind for herself, too. But why Flint's temporary stay in Red Rock caused her a twinge of regret, Jessie didn't know.

Still, she was focused on her kids—exactly where she wanted her focus to be—and she ignored it.

"I hope he goes home soon," Ella grumbled.

"I don't!" Bethany countered. "I like him!"

"I *love* 'im!" Adam said, not to be outdone.

"You do not *love* him," Ella insisted. "We *loved* Daddy. Flint is just a big fat—"

"Flint is a perfectly nice man," Jessie cut her eldest off before Ella went off on a tangent. "And he's a guest when he's with us. So we can have fun with him and enjoy his company—and we need to treat him the way we treat guests—" she said pointedly to Ella "—but I want you all to be clear that that's all he is. A friend. A visitor. A guest."

"And he's gonna leave sometime," Ella said, apparently needing to hang on to that.

"And, yes," Jessie confirmed, "he will leave."

"I'm gonna ast 'im to stay for-eber." Another of Adam's decrees.

"I want him to stay," Braden said.

"Me, too," Bethany added as if they all had a vote.

Jessie sighed, then she repeated herself for effect. "Flint doesn't live here. He's only visiting. We need to be nice to him. You can enjoy spending time with him while he's here. But I want you all not to forget that he won't be here for long."

"Good!" Ella managed to get in at the same time Jessie's mother called for the kids to bring their laundry downstairs the way she'd asked them to.

"Go on and tell Gramma I'll be there in a few minutes," Jessie urged.

"We still gets to see Fwint tonight," she heard Adam mutter to Braden and Bethany as they got off her bed.

"Too bad!" Ella couldn't seem to resist putting in just before the four of them left Jessie's bedroom.

Jessie just hoped that she'd gotten through to them about Flint—and that her words might entice Ella to be nice.

But she had to admit that if truth be told, she wasn't sure on which side of the Flint-leaving issue she would cast her own vote.

Because while she knew he *would* be leaving soon and that it was for the best, because she couldn't seem to contain her attraction to him, there was also a part of her that was clinging to every single minute she got to spend with him. A part of her that couldn't help feeling a little like Adam, Bethany and Braden did about how terrific he was.

A part of her that wanted him to stay around, too, probably more than her hero-worshipping kids did.

But for such different reasons.

* * *

"Hang on just a minute."

Game night had been enough of a success that Jessie thought she'd even seen Ella fight a smile or two during the course of it. But Kelsey and Coop had taken Anthony home an hour earlier, the last of the popcorn and cookies had been eaten, and her parents had offered to put the kids to bed while Jessie cleaned up downstairs. That was when Flint halted the process of urging Adam, Braden, Bethany and Ella to their rooms.

"I didn't want to distract them from their fun before, but I brought them each something," Flint said to Jessie when she tossed him a quizzical glance.

"Presents?" Adam said excitedly.

"Just a little something," Flint said.

Jessie had seen her sister slip him a brown paper sack from Anthony's diaper bag just before they'd left, but she'd had no idea what was in it. Flint had discreetly set it alongside the easy chair he'd been sitting in to play Candy Land. Now Flint had the sack in hand as three of her kids charged him and Ella looked on with barely veiled curiosity from a distance.

Flint opened the bag and took a small replica of a totem pole from it.

"Adam, this is for you—it's a totem pole to watch over you."

"It gots a face like a man with a bird thingy for a nose," the three-year-old marveled.

"The *thingy* is a beak," Jessie said from where she looked on as curiously as Ella did.

"Can I play wis it, too?"

"You can. You can ward off all sorts of aliens and attackers with that," Flint assured before he took a beaded bracelet out for Bethany.

"This will bring you good luck, Bethany, and I thought the beads were the color of your pretty eyes," he said to the four-year-old.

"Look, Mama, are they the color my eyes are?"

"They are," Jessie assured, watching her daughter beam.

"This is for Braden," Flint said then, taking out a small, leather-wrapped hoop with webbing laced on the inside like an ornate spiderweb. "This is a dream catcher," he explained. "If you put it near your bed it should help to catch some of the bad dreams before they can come to you in your sleep, so you won't have so many of them."

"Is that true, Mama?" Braden asked hopefully.

"I think we should give it a try," Jessie said somberly, hoping anything would work.

"And last but not least," Flint said as he handed the dream catcher to Braden and took a very small hand-painted oval box from the lunch sack, "this is for Ella."

The seven-year-old still might not have liked him, but she couldn't resist a gift. Showing some reluctance, she stepped up and accepted it.

"What is it?"

"Open the box," Flint advised.

When she did, she removed tiny stick dolls wrapped in brightly colored string.

"They're Worry People," Flint explained. "You can give all your troubles to them, put them under your pillow when you sleep and forget everything that's bothering you so you can rest."

Ella frowned suspiciously but seemed intrigued nonetheless. And to her credit, without her mother's encouragement, she said a very solemn, "Thank you," as if she had need to share her burdens and actually was grateful. Which made Jessie's heart ache just a little.

But all she could do was remind her other children to thank Flint before her parents finally did get them to go upstairs with their new treasures.

"That was very nice of you," she told Flint when everyone was gone. Nice and touching and so thoughtful of him to have personalized each gift to each child. "You didn't have to do that."

"I did it because I wanted to," he said, using the empty bag as a trash receptacle to collect stray popcorn kernels and discarded napkins. As he did, Jessie tried not to notice for the millionth time tonight that the man could rock a pair of jeans like nobody's business.

But it wasn't easy.

Still, she tore her eyes away from his derriere and began to gather plates, bowls and glasses as Flint said, "I had nightmares as a kid. I hated to hear that Braden is suffering through that. And Ella… I think Ella has more worries than she should have. I wasn't sure what to do for Adam and Bethany, so I just played it safe."

"It was still really nice," she said. Then, even though she had no desire to see him go, she said, "You don't have to help with this stuff, too. If you want to get home or if you have somewhere else to be…"

"Actually, I was kind of hoping that if we got this cleared away in a hurry I might be able to talk you into showing me your studio."

"Oh, you don't want to see that," Jessie demurred self-consciously.

"Yes, I do. What do you say? Can I earn my way into a private showing by emptying the trash?" He held up the small sack he'd been filling and she drank in the sight of him in a form-fitting white crew-necked T-shirt that accentuated his muscular, V-shaped torso divinely.

And between how appealing he looked, the fact that he always managed to lighten her mood, and having brought her kids such kind and caring gifts, how could she say no to him?

"Okay, but don't have high expectations. I took art in middle and high school, but I've taken only a few adult classes at night school over the years, so it isn't as if I'm trained or anything. I'm just a putterer."

"Then I want to see your putterings."

"Why don't you work on clearing up the games while I do the dishes, then I'll show you my putterings?"

Had that come out sounding suggestive?

It had to her.

And it must have to him because he grinned devilishly.

But he also must have realized that she hadn't intended to say anything suggestive because he let her off the hook with a simple, "It's a deal."

She took the paper bag he offered and the dinnerware she'd stacked into the kitchen. With the trash disposed of, she stood at the sink to rinse the dishes and put them in the dishwasher.

As she did, she took stock of her own appearance in her reflection of the window above the sink.

She was wearing jeans, too, and a simple navy blue shirt that she'd chosen for the princess seams that allowed the blouse to hug her curves just a bit. Luckily she'd managed to spend an entire evening with her kids without having anything spilled on her, so there were no spots to worry about.

She'd twisted her hair into a French knot in the back and left the ends to erupt in a bundle of curls at her crown, and that was still neat and tidy. And although the dark glass didn't reflect too many details, she thought the lip gloss she'd reapplied after dinner had stayed on and she didn't see any mascara smudges under her eyes.

Not that it mattered how she looked, she told herself. This had been a purely aboveboard family game night that would end with her showing Flint her rock sculptures before he went home. Simple as that. Without any kind of good-night kiss being called for because this hadn't been a date.

Of course, yesterday's rock-collecting outing had also been a family event and not a date.

But still, she lectured herself, she needed to not let anything develop between herself and Flint.

And yet the fact that Flint had hung back when he could have left earlier with Kelsey and Cooper or when the kids went up to bed… Well, did that mean he'd had a plan for getting a few minutes alone with her?

Jessie couldn't stifle the little rush of excitement at that thought.

And that little rush of excitement felt so good.

"All done. How about you?"

Jessie startled at Flint's voice, but recovered quickly.

"I'm done, too," she said, turning off the water and closing the dishwasher.

"Then lead me to the putterings."

He'd put a wicked twist to the word that time and

she knew he'd done it on purpose to tease her. It made her smile, but she didn't acknowledge his goading; she merely led him out the rear door.

As they crossed the yard—careful to step around the jungle gym parts and pieces that had yet to be put together—Jessie said, "When we rented the apartment it was furnished and everything is still in it, just pushed against the walls. It looks kind of messy—"

"I've never been in an art studio that didn't look messy."

"I'm just saying that it's kind of a mishmash."

When they reached the studio, Jessie opened the door and flipped on the light. She went in ahead of Flint.

The space wasn't large and with the exception of a bathroom and closet at the far end, it was just one big open room with the separate sections defined by the small refrigerator, stove and sink against one wall; a double bed and dresser near the bathroom and closet end; and a sofa, easy chair and two end tables riding the wall that ran beside the door.

When Jessie had taken it over as an art studio she'd added a huge worktable smack-dab in the center of the place. The worktable was laden with stones and supplies, while sections of the floor, all the counters, the small kitchen table, the end tables and every shelf of the bookcase held finished sculptures.

"Ta-da!" she said with forced flourish as she crossed the space to flip another switch and flood the place with even more light.

She'd shown her sculptures to people other than family and friends before, and while she was never completely comfortable with it, it hadn't ever made her feel as vulnerable as she did now. But there was no stopping

Flint as he began to examine her work with all the somber study of an art lover at the Louvre.

Her discomfort wouldn't allow her to keep quiet, though, so she said, "It's sort of like people who put up easels in the countryside and paint landscapes—I see rock formations and waterfalls and things in the woods, and then come home and try to reproduce them. Like little pieces of nature that can be brought indoors."

Flint nodded that handsome head of his, but he wouldn't be distracted from studying sculpture after sculpture.

And Jessie still couldn't merely stand there and watch him.

"The kids and I wash most of the rocks," she continued to babble. "But if we've found some with moss growing on them, I wait till any mud or dirt is dry enough to brush off so I can leave the moss undisturbed—I think it adds a little something. And a few of the pieces have water—a guy at the hobby shop showed me how I could hide small reservoirs in some of them and pump the water up and over the top like waterfalls."

"This one?" Flint asked, pointing to the first of those that he'd reached. "Will you show me?"

She went to where he was standing and leaned in front of him to turn on the water feature, catching a whiff of his cologne as she did, and making her all the more aware of him and the effect he had on her. It didn't help her composure.

Which launched her into more chatter.

"The kids love it when I use the rocks they've picked up. They feel like they have their own part in the sculptures. Of course sometimes that means they get competitive and insist that the sculpture with their particular rocks are better than the other ones and then I take the brunt of it because they'll say the other ones are ugly."

"I don't see anything ugly here," Flint said without taking his eyes off her work. And the fact that he sounded as if he genuinely meant it gave her a tiny wave of elation.

"Kelsey chose that one as a housewarming gift," she said when he had circled the entire place and ended at the door where she'd set another of the fountain sculptures on the end table there. "I thought I'd bring it on Sunday to the party. So, now that I think of it, I guess you would have seen what I do with the rocks then..."

"I'm glad I didn't have to wait."

Flint had seen how to turn on the water on the other fountain and so he did it with the one that would be Kelsey and Coop's.

Jessie busied herself shutting down the first one.

"You really don't know what you have here, do you?" he asked then.

"A whole bunch of rock piles?" Jessie joked as she pivoted in his direction, watching him watch the miniature wall of water cascade over moss rocks into a replica of a pond that was lined with mica rock to reflect blues and greens from beneath and make the water appear to shimmer.

"These are beautiful," he declared.

Then he stopped the water feature on the sculpture and switched his focus to Jessie, catching her staring as he crossed to her big square worktable.

"Honestly," he said as he did. "They're beautiful."

"Thanks," she responded quietly to his reiteration of the compliment, ill at ease with it.

There were bar stools around the worktable that she

sat on when she worked, that the kids used when they came to watch her. Flint perched a hip on one of them, stretching a long leg far out from it and hooking his other boot heel over the front rung, obviously having no intention of leaving now that they'd done what they'd come out there to do.

Not that Jessie was sorry to see that. Much as she knew she should avoid it, a little time alone with him seemed like a treat…a reward. So she joined him, sitting around the corner from him so she could face him.

Flint used his index finger to indicate the three un-occupied bar stools. "Do you have help putting your sculptures together?"

Jessie laughed. "No, but sometimes I have an audience. I think the kids come here when I'm working because it's like a session with a therapist for them. So even when I think that the income from renting the place again would help give me a cushion, I don't do it because the money isn't as important as the closeness I get from that alone time with the kids when they come out here with me on their own to talk. Sometimes I get to see a whole different side to them."

"But all this—" Flint motioned to the rock sculptures on the table. "This shows that their mom has a whole other side herself. An alter ego who's an artist. And they get to see that."

Back to being embarrassed. "I don't think of myself as an artist."

"You should. I'm telling you, these are really wonderful. So why don't you let this space make you some money after all?"

"You lost me," Jessie said, frowning in confusion.

"Why not sell the sculptures?"

She laughed and something about that caused him to smile.

"I'm serious, Jessie," he said, his eyes so intently on her that she was afraid she might blush. "These are good. *You're* good. I know I can either sell them outright to some of the shops I deal with or place them in a few of the galleries for sale."

"No," she demurred in disbelief. "They're just…my little rock piles."

Flint chuckled at that. "Your *little rock piles* are intricate and multifaceted little natural wonders of their own. Haven't you ever sold one?"

"I don't even give them away unless someone asks for one. I don't want anyone to have to hide them in a closet and then try to remember to take them out when I visit to make me think they don't hate the weird gift I gave them."

Flint shook his head. "I'm telling you that I can sell them. Why don't you let me put out some feelers and prove it to you?"

Flattered, Jessie was still hesitant. She found it difficult to believe that her sculptures were as good as he said and could actually bring in money.

But there was another facet to his suggestion—doing business with Flint would mean more of a continuing connection with him.

And in the midst of her strongest attractions to him, her most potent fantasies about him, her daydreams and inability to stop thinking about him almost every waking minute, it was the fact that he wouldn't be staying in Red Rock that made that all seem not so dangerous. The fact that he would leave and that from then on her contact with him would be rare, gave her hope that what seemed like it might be a tiny crush on him would just resolve itself.

But if he sold her sculptures?

There would definitely be maintained contact. And it wouldn't merely be from a distance on an occasional visit he might make to his brother next door. It would be a continuing arrangement just between the two of them. Complete with the potential that she would go on harboring this ever-growing attraction to him while he dropped in, poured fuel on the fire, and then sauntered out again to get on with the rest of his life.

That didn't seem like something that would be good for her in the long run. So she tried to decline.

"No, I don't think so," she said.

"Jessie, you could be sitting on Ella's entire college education right here in this room."

"Come on, that isn't true," she said, actually leery of believing that, because putting anything in terms of her kids was her weakest spot and she knew it would be all the more difficult to resist what he was suggesting.

"It is true," he insisted. "You can make some serious bank here, lady."

"I can't believe that."

He reached across the corner of her worktable and took her hand, rubbing the back of it with his thumb. "Like I said, let me prove it to you. Let me take some pictures of the pieces and show them to my people. If I'm right—"

"If you're wrong it will be humiliating."

He smiled gently, patiently. "I'm not wrong. I know my business, my buyers, my market. And when I come back to you with facts and figures, *then* you can tell me what you want to do. Or not."

He could be wrong, Jessie thought. Which would solve the problem. Or if he was right, by the time what he was proposing actually happened, maybe she would have found some fatal flaw in him that totally turned her off. And any amount of contact she might have to have with him wouldn't matter...because he wouldn't be so enticing.

"You don't have anything to lose," he said.

His hand was big and strong and warm, and hers seemed to fit into it as if it were made to be there. Plus his eyes were holding hers so tenderly that they were making it impossible not to trust him.

And heaven help her, she heard herself say, "Okay, you can take pictures. Then we'll see."

Flint grinned and Jessie felt much, much too happy to have pleased him.

"You won't be sorry," he promised, squeezing her hand, still gazing into her eyes, making her think for the millionth time about that kiss they'd shared the night before.

Then he let go of her hand and got up from the bar stool, and Jessie had the oddest yen to reach out and take his hand back, to keep him from leaving.

Of course she didn't do that. Instead, as she stood, too, she heard him say, "We've been warned that tomorrow will be jam-packed—"

"Right. Everything needs to be finished, the house needs to be cleaned, and we have to get set up for the housewarming party on Sunday," Jessie confirmed.

"So I'd better let you get some rest. I heard Kelsey tell you to come over at seven tomorrow morning."

"We're even putting the kids and Mom and Dad to work, but they'll be over later."

While Flint went to the studio door and opened it, Jessie turned off the light switch on the opposite wall. Just as she was joining him at the door he flipped off that light switch, too.

The moon was nearly full and very bright, illuminating the dark studio.

"This is kind of like being out in the woods with you again," Flint said.

He was standing in the doorway, facing the shelves inside. Jessie took a look over her shoulder at what he was seeing as her backdrop. Somehow the stone sculptures drank in the moonlight and reflected it back, making them stand out in the milky glow more than any of the furniture.

"I suppose if you put enough of them around it *is* like being out in the forest," she agreed.

"Only here I get you all to myself. I'm beginning to see the appeal of the studio."

Jessie wasn't too sure what to say to that. And because he was blocking the exit she couldn't get past him to go outside. So there she was, standing in the moon glow, facing Flint.

And again thinking about that kiss from the night before.

"Early day tomorrow," she said in a voice far softer and more breathy than she'd intended it to be.

"Early day tomorrow and I should get going. I shouldn't be..." He muttered to himself as he took a step toward her, raised that same big, strong hand that had held hers earlier and placed it gently to the side of her face.

She had to tilt her head up to see him when he closed the distance between them. Or at least that's what she told herself, not wanting to admit that the movement could also be interpreted as an invitation. And certainly letting his hand stay on her face was not a rebuff, even though in her mind she was checking off the reasons why she shouldn't let this happen again and adding to the list the fact that they could be working together in the future.

But his fingertips were in her hair, his palm followed the curve of her jaw, and the scent of his cologne went right to her head. And in the backdrop of moonlight his dark handsomeness was all the more stark.

So when he leaned in, when his mouth first pressed to hers, all those reasons fled, her eyes closed, and she just gave herself over to that kiss that she'd been wishing for since the moment the last one had ended.

This kiss was different though. Flint's lips lingered, parting over hers, beckoning hers to part, too. And when his big hand caressed her face and pulled her closer, that kiss grew deeper and deeper.

On its own, her hand rose to his chest, feeling the hardness of honed muscle that his white T-shirt hinted at, and Jessie immersed herself for a moment in the feel of him as he went on kissing her so soundly that she couldn't think about anything else.

His other arm went around her, pulling her nearer with a hand splayed against her back. Even as she was drawn in by his strengths, she considered that she was alone in a dark, somewhat secluded place with him. Kissing him, letting him kiss her. Giving signs of encouragement that she knew shouldn't be given....

Maybe there was something in her response that sent that message, because he suddenly took his arm away and gave her more breathing room. It was only a moment before he brought it to an end, before they were merely standing there in the moonlight again, his hand still on her cheek.

"Early day tomorrow," he said, belatedly parroting her words.

Jessie nodded, her lips still tingling from that kiss. That kiss that—even though she'd initiated ending it— she wished he would start all over again.

But he slowly drew his hand from her cheek, stopping before he'd abandoned it completely to cup her chin, tilt it upward once more, and kiss her again, more gently this time.

Then he stepped through the door, waiting outside for her to follow.

Which she did—a split second after winning a battle with her inclination to yank him back into the studio for more kissing.

"I'll go through the gate," Flint said as Jessie set off for her house.

She paused when she realized he wasn't going with her, that he was pointing to the gate that connected her yard and Kelsey's.

"Okay. Then I'll just see you tomorrow," she said.

"Bright and early," Flint confirmed as he aimed for the fence.

Jessie went the rest of the way to her house, glancing over her shoulder as she opened the screen door to see Flint headed for her sister's place—tall, straight-backed and broad-shouldered.

And she was wishing with a horrible ferocity that he'd walked her to her door and kissed her at least once more, which was when she knew that she definitely had a crush on the man.

A crush that she needed to squelch.

But that wasn't shaping up to be an easy task.

Not when it seemed resilient enough to even grow under the onslaught of her widow's guilt, her devotion to her kids and the sure and certain knowledge that there was no future for a mother of four with a man like Flint.

Chapter Seven

On Saturday morning. Jessie went to her sister's house at 7:00 a.m. sharp. While Flint, Coop and eventually Jessie's father finished construction details and cleanup, Jessie, Kelsey, the kids and Jeannie cleaned, vacuumed, hung curtains and pictures and arranged furniture before using the evening to get things set up for Sunday's housewarming party.

At about nine o'clock that evening Flint's services were no longer needed and when Coop let him off the hook from party preparations, Flint went upstairs to shower. By the time he was finished, Kelsey had suggested that Jessie take her four very tired kids home and call it a day, too. Jeannie and Jack assured Jessie that they would stay and help Kelsey and Coop, encouraging Jessie to go.

And when Flint offered his help in taking the kids

home and putting them to bed…? Adam literally jumped for joy, Bethany and Braden chimed in with their approval, all four other adults enthusiastically supported the idea, and Jessie was too worn-out to argue.

Not that she had any inclination to, despite the fact that she knew she should. The day had been so busy that she and Flint had barely crossed paths or exchanged glances, and while that should have been just fine, she somehow felt cheated. No amount of reasoning with herself changed that; and while his assistance in putting four kids to bed was still not exactly the sort of togetherness she had in mind, she wasn't going to pass up the opportunity to have even a few more minutes with him.

So off they went to Jessie's house, as she tried not to think that any outsider looking in might have thought that they were a family.

She didn't typically give the kids communal baths, but because it was long past their bedtimes and she was beat, she dispatched the boys to one tub and the girls to the other. Flint kept an eye on the boys, while Jessie ran between bathrooms to actually oversee and aid the bathing.

Flint cleaned out the tubs while Jessie tidied up after the kids.

Then he made a suggestion.

"I can crack the whip with the teeth brushing and read the bedtime story. Why don't you go shower?"

"Do I look that bad?" she joked. She knew that she did look the worse for wear, that her hair was stringy, the light makeup she'd applied that morning was long gone and her clothes were smudged and dirty.

Flint just grinned in response.

Of course there was the possibility that he had come home with her solely to help with the kids and would disappear the minute those services were rendered. Jessie couldn't blame him if he did, because he had also worked like a dog all day and evening. And while his shower had washed away the grime and left his hair slightly damp, and he'd put on a clean pair of jeans and a plain white T-shirt, he hadn't gone so far as to shave the dark shadow of beard that had reappeared as the day and evening had worn on, which seemed like a dead giveaway that he didn't have too much energy left either.

But if there was any chance that he might stick around, that she might have even a few minutes alone with him before her parents returned, Jessie didn't want to spend those few minutes grubby herself.

So in regard to his offer to finish the final steps to getting the kids to bed while she showered, she said, "You're sure?"

He looked her up and down, laughed and said jokingly, "Oh yeah, I'm sure."

Jessie made a face and threw a wet washcloth at him.

He caught it. "Go on before any of that dirt sticks."

Jessie dispatched Ella to help Adam brush his teeth, promised she'd be only a few minutes and would still tuck them all in, and made a beeline for the shower in the bathroom connected to her bedroom, shedding clothes the minute she was behind her closed door.

She took the fastest shower she could and did the quickest shampoo, too. But not merely to make sure she could say good-night to her children. She knew her parents wouldn't be at Kelsey's house for too much longer and if she was going to get any time at all alone with Flint, she had to hurry.

Lecturing herself all the while about the lack of wisdom in giving in to her whims when it came to this man, she nevertheless toweled herself off, flipped her head upside down to give her hair five minutes of blow-drying, brushed on just enough blush to camouflage her fatigue, did a swipe of mascara to each eye and pulled on a hoodie that she left unzipped just half an inch lower than usual and the yoga pants that she knew cupped her rear end to perfection but would still make it look as if she'd just thrown something on.

Then, with one quick glance at herself in the mirror, with too many vivid memories of last night's kisses still swirling in her brain, she rejoined the group.

"And that was when Ella the Magnificent, Bethany the Bold, Braden the Brave and Atomic Adam saved all the baby bears and brought them home to their family."

"We did it! That wuz us's!" Adam shouted, jumping up and down on the foot of Braden's bed where Adam, Braden and Bethany were gathered around Flint. Ella looked on from more of a distance, perched on Adam's bed on the other side of the nightstand that separated the matching twin-size beds.

From the doorway, Jessie watched her oldest daughter go from being spellbound by whatever story Flint had just told back to a show of disdain for how enthralled her brothers and sister were.

"It was just a story," Ella insisted to Adam.

"It was a good one!" Braden said.

"I liked that I was pretty." Bethany giggled. "And you were pretty, too, El!"

Jessie watched her oldest poke her chin in the air as if that meant nothing to her, but it was clear that Ella was as delighted as Bethany by whatever characterization Flint had bestowed upon her.

It might not be happening with any kind of speed, but Jessie thought that Flint was slowly inching into Ella's good graces. Very slowly, dragged down by Ella's reluctance to let it happen, but inching nonetheless.

Adam was still jumping on the bed, so Jessie went the rest of the way into the bedroom. "You know better than to jump on the bed, Adam," she scolded.

"I'm 'tomic Adam!" Adam corrected. "I can shoot arrows outta my fumbs!" Two thumbs-up seemed to prove that, but the three-year-old did stop jumping on the bed.

"I can turn everything into ice with my eyes," Braden announced.

"I can run faster than a rocket and jump higher than big buildings and I'm not 'fraid of nothin'!" Bethany claimed.

"And Ella is like the mama wion," Adam said in awe. "Hers fingernails can turn into big long claws and she doesn't let no bad guys hurt no good guys 'cause she per'tects ever'body!"

"Wow," Jessie marveled, catching Adam when he leaped into her arms just as she reached the bed. "That sounds like quite a story."

"It was the bestest!" Adam proclaimed, clearly none of his hero worship of Flint abated.

"But now you're all riled up just when it's time to

go to sleep," Jessie said pointedly, pinning Flint with her gaze.

He grinned and said to his entourage, "What happens after a big rescue mission?"

"We're all worn-out and we need to rest, so we have to go right to bed," Bethany seemed to quote.

"I'm ready," Ella said as if she'd been bored to tears. "Come on, Bethany, let's go to our room."

Jessie's house had four bedrooms. Hers was the master bedroom, her parents were in the guest bedroom, and the other two—including the one they were in—were shared by the children: boys in one, girls in the other.

Apparently the condition in the story about going to bed right after a rescue had stuck because Bethany scooted off Braden's bed on command and said, "G'night, Flint."

"Good night, Bethany the Bold. Sleep tight."

As Ella led her sister out of the room she obviously had no intention of saying anything to Flint, so Jessie said, "Ella, what do you say?"

"'Night," she grumbled.

"'Night, Ella," Flint responded as if the seven-year-old had been perfectly gracious.

"I'll be in in a minute," Jessie called after them. Then she lay Adam down on his mattress.

"The baws keeps me from faw'in out," he explained as he peered at Flint through the safety bars that guarded the upper half of his mattress.

"Good idea," Flint said, giving his approval as he got off Braden's bed so Braden could get under the covers.

"When Aunt Kelsey mayw-wees Coop," Adam announced then, "Ella and Beth'ny are gonna be the flower girls, and me and Braden's gonna be the ring barrels."

"Bringing up a new topic—that's a stall tactic," Jessie warned Flint when she saw him being drawn in. "And he means ring *bearers,* not *barrels.*"

To Adam she said, "No more talking now. It's time to go to sleep. Tomorrow is another big day."

"Will Fwint be there?"

"Yes, he will be. So you can see him then."

Appeased and exhausted, Adam snatched the stuffed floppy dog he slept with and began his nightly ritual of rubbing the dog's ear against his cheek. Jessie leaned over the safety bars and kissed her youngest's forehead.

Then she tucked in Braden and kissed him as well. Like his twin, Braden bid Flint good-night without prompting.

"Two down, two to go," Jessie said as they left the room, pulling the door halfway closed.

"But probably Ella would rather I not be in on your saying good-night to her," Flint guessed. "I'm craving a little cool night air, though. Think you can stay awake for a while longer to join me on the porch?"

Far more delighted than she wanted to be—and all too willing to ignore how tired she was—Jessie said, "Front porch or back?"

"I'll be waiting for you on the back," he promised.

And then he did something that Jessie thought was purely out of some kind of reflex—he ran a parting hand down her back.

It took her by surprise. It seemed to take him by surprise, too, because he pulled his hand away almost immediately.

But still the contact was inviting, hinting at a forbidden intimacy, and it sent tiny tingles up and down her spine.

It's exhaustion, she told herself. That was what had caused him to forget himself and rub her back. That was what had allowed such a simple, short-lived thing to thrill her.

And she honestly thought both of those things were true.

But it still didn't keep her from making quick work of tucking in the girls so that she could get outside to Flint.

When Jessie made it to the back porch, her parents were already there, chatting with Flint, apparently having just returned from Kelsey's.

The disappointment that Jessie felt at that first realization that she and Flint were no longer alone deflated her. But after a brief exchange of small talk Jack and Jeannie admitted to their own weariness, said goodnight and went inside.

And finally Jessie was alone with Flint.

He sat on the landing so one long leg could stretch down onto the grass while he bent the other at the knee. He leaned into the gap in the porch railing that accommodated the stairs. Then he patted the space in front of him—an invitation.

It didn't take more than that for Jessie to join him. Her own feet landed flat on the bottom step and she hugged her thighs, resting her head on her knees to look at Flint as he studied her with an approving, appreciative expression on his scruffily whiskered face.

"Definitely an improvement," he said, obviously referring to the results of her own shower.

"Feels better, too," she agreed.

For a moment then neither of them said anything and to Jessie it seemed as if they were finally winding down, relaxing. But it surprised her to realize that she could feel comfortable with silence between them. It had taken much longer for her and Pete to achieve that.

But just as she was beginning to consider how to break that silence, Flint saved her the effort.

"The murals on the kids' walls," he said. "The cartoon cars and trucks and trains in the boys' room, and the fairies and gnomes and unicorns in that whole garden scene in the girls'—Braden said you painted those."

"I did. Over the winter."

Flint shook his head, his forehead beetled in what appeared to be perplexity. "You're amazing."

"Why?"

"Because the work is amazing."

"It's no big deal. It was just fun."

"Okay, I headed down this road a little last night but didn't get too far, and tonight I really need to know. Not the mom, not the wife or widow, just you—"

Jessie laughed. "It's all *just* me."

"Tell me what you were like in the pre-marriage, pre-kids days. When you were a girl. Were you always interested in art? Did you want to grow up and become an artist?"

She merely laughed again. "I always liked to draw and paint and make things, but it was just something I liked to do."

"Well, whether you know it or not," he decreed, "you're an artist."

Jessie merely made a face at that notion.

"So what *did* you want to be?" he asked.

She shrugged. "Kelsey always loved animals—particularly horses—which made her more down to earth, I think. But me? I was the dreamer. The romantic. I never thought of *being* something when I grew up, which I regret. I just always pictured falling in love, getting married, having babies, a home. It was family that I saw for myself, not a career. Even though I guess that's old-fashioned."

"And you regret it?"

She was quiet for a moment. "Regret isn't the right word. It would just be a lot more helpful now if I'd gone to college, if I had a degree, if I had put some time and energy—and thought—into having a career, too. The most I thought of in that direction was that yes, I'd probably need to work—as maybe a receptionist or in an office or a store or something that I could do full-time until I had kids. Then maybe part-time after that to just bring in a second income for the family I wanted. I knew exactly the kind of wedding I wanted to have, the kind of house. I wanted to be a good cook, have a garden. But when it came to making a living? Like I said, my plans were all tinted with romance."

"What career would you have chosen if you'd gone to college?"

"I've wondered that same thing. Psychology, I think."

Something about that made him smile. "Not art? Really? When you're so good?"

"You're stuck on that, aren't you? But, no. I told you, art has always been just for fun."

"So psychology, then—which I guess makes sense

because you're already doing armchair therapy at your worktable in the studio. But why psychology?"

He seemed to genuinely want to know. To know just about her and the person she was. It had been so long since anyone had seen her as anything but a wife, a widow, a mom that it was strange. Nice. But strange.

"I guess I like to know what makes people tick," she said. "I'm always trying to understand the motivation behind what people do, the way they are."

"Have you ever thought about going back to college now?'

Jessie's laugh at that sounded almost tipsy because she was so tired. "There's no way."

"Why not? It isn't too late. People go back to school at all ages."

"But I have four kids. It would take too much away from them for me to go off in a new direction, to need to concentrate on something else, and I wouldn't do that."

"So it's back to the family thing. You really are into that."

"I really am," she said firmly. "What about you?" she asked then. "What was the younger version of Flint like? What did you want to be? Or do you have exactly the life you wanted, the life you thought you'd have?"

He smiled at her. "I didn't put any planning into anything but getting out of the chaos that was growing up with Cindy Fortune. I didn't think about a career either. I just thought about a job, what I could do that would make some money so I could be out on my own—which I was the day after I graduated high school. And since then, when it comes to life, to occupations, I've just gone where the wind blew me, tried to learn from things along the way, adjust so I don't make the same mistakes in life twice."

Somehow Jessie didn't think he was only talking about jobs when he said that, but she was too exhausted to delve into anything overly serious at that moment. She was just enjoying the evening air. And Flint.

The porch light was off to not attract bugs; there was only a dim light over the kitchen sink that cast a slight glow through the window. But the moonlight, like the night before, illuminated Flint's achingly masculine features and made her heart beat quicken just from looking at him.

She sat up straight, with her back against the opposite post, resisting the thoughts that came with that faster pulse and brought her once again to the kiss that had ended their evening the previous night.

Flint was still watching her, and in the midst of it a small smile spread across that face that Jessie just couldn't take her eyes off.

"What?" she asked about the cause of that smile.

"I was just thinking that you'd be good as a psychologist because you're easy to talk to, to confide in. I'd tell you my troubles…"

"Do you have troubles?" she asked.

"I do. Just lately," he said in a way that let her know he wasn't being serious—or was he? "There's this person, who shall remain nameless, who's really distracting me. I'm having problems thinking about anything else. I even dreamed about her last night."

"Ah, dreams can be very revealing," Jessie said like a carnival fortune-teller.

Flint grinned. "Well, this one was a doozy but it didn't reveal nearly enough."

"In what way?" Jessie asked, intrigued even though she knew they were just playing.

Flint pointed his chin in the direction of Kelsey's house next door. "The room I'm staying in has a window that faces the bedroom window of this Person-Who-Shall-Remain-Nameless. In the dream I was standing there, it was late at night, quiet…" His voice went quiet, too. "The only light on anywhere was in that other bedroom across the way. And behind the closed curtains I could just make out her silhouette."

"That didn't actually happen, did it?" Jessie asked, a little alarmed to think that maybe he'd been watching her from his window, that he *had* seen her silhouetted against the curtains.

Her concern made him grin. "No, it didn't actually happen. But could it?" he requested incorrigibly.

"No, it could not!" Jessie reprimanded with a laugh. Then she said, "And I'm ready to give you my expert psychological evaluation—you're a sick, sick man," she joked.

"I can't help myself," he confessed. "There's just something about this person that's gotten into my system."

He came away from the post to lean more toward her, reaching for her hands with both of his, staring down at them while he said, "I just really, really…*like* you."

That made her smile—and feel a whole lot of things that were dangerous for her to be feeling.

Then he glanced up from his study of their intertwined hands and gazed into her eyes for a moment before he leaned just an inch or two closer, clearly aiming to kiss her.

But instead he paused, waiting, as if this time he

wouldn't do it unless she met him halfway, unless she let him know that it was something she wanted him to do.

She wished she didn't. But wishing didn't make it so. She wanted for him to kiss her so badly that she couldn't keep from drifting an inch or two forward herself, raising her chin almost imperceptibly but enough to give permission.

Permission he didn't hesitate to accept—kissing her once more with his lips parted from the start, and heat waiting just below the surface, as if he'd been thinking about this as much as she had.

One of his hands released one of hers to rise up into her hair, to cup the back of her head as he opened his mouth a bit wider and let that kiss deepen.

Jessie recalled too vividly what it had been like to feel his chest through his shirt the previous night and she yearned to feel it again. So that was where her free hand went—to a hard wall of pectoral.

He placed her other hand there, too, before he wrapped an arm around her and pulled her nearer still.

Mouths were somehow open much wider by then and that was when Flint's tongue flicked hers, bold and brazen and titillating at once.

It sent more than a little shockwave through her, though, exciting her even as she felt a tiny spark of guilt to be indulging in such a moment of familiarity with someone other than Pete.

But somehow that tiny spark of guilt burned out a split second later, overtaken by a kiss that was growing hotter and hotter by the minute.

Tongues toyed and teased and tantalized, and even more sensations awakened in her as she let one hand course upward into Flint's hair, as she learned the nuances of his kiss and tried a few tricks of her own that only added to the heat that was building between them.

That heat was building in her, too, making her suddenly much, much too aware of the feel of her nipples hardened against the cups of her bra. That made her imagine Flint's hands there, imagine them cupping her breasts, massaging, caressing them instead of the back of her head, her shoulders...

Maybe exhaustion had lowered their inhibitions, Jessie thought, recalling the way Flint had unconsciously run his hand down her back earlier. Maybe it had reduced them to baser instincts.

And if she let it continue, she was afraid of where it might go from there. Where it might end.

But, oh, that kiss!

She didn't want to put a stop to it. She wanted to go on kissing him, to feel the touch of his hand on her bare skin.

But she wanted it all so much that she knew she was fast losing control. That whether it was fatigue or not, her defenses were down, and she just couldn't keep at this and not have it go further than it already had.

So reluctantly she drew her hand from the side of his neck, bringing it down to his chest again, where she gave the slightest push as she forced her tongue to shy away from his just slightly. Just enough to send a message.

A message that seemed to be received, pondered, then answered with one more bold thrust of his tongue to let her know he wasn't any more eager than she was to stop before he honored those silent clues and brought that kiss to a slow conclusion.

Jessie opened her eyes to find his still closed even as he helped her sit up again. His eyebrows arched before he finally opened his eyes as if from a dream like the one he'd teased her with earlier, making him look very much like he needed to regain his bearings, his senses.

Then, in a deep, raspy voice that had a hint of humor to it, he repeated, "I just really, really like you," as if a reason for that kiss had been called for.

"Maybe you should stop it," Jessie managed to joke amidst the struggle to calm all that he'd stirred in her.

"Easier said than done," he whispered.

Then he slipped both his hands into her hair on either side of her head and held her to another kiss. And while his tongue stayed contained, it was still a long, lingering, cherishing kind of kiss that threatened to put them right back where they'd been a moment before.

But this time Flint didn't let that happen, stopping to kiss her once more, then again, then again, until he seemed to be spent and let go of her.

That was when he got to his feet and moved into the backyard, out of arm's reach.

"Good night, Jess," he said as if there was nothing else to say.

"Good night, Flint," Jessie whispered in return.

She watched him walk with a sexy swagger across the grass to the fence, her gaze riding every rise and fall of his denim-clad derriere.

She watched him go through the gate, go up to Kelsey's house and in the back door, tonight not casting her one final glance or wave.

That was when Jessie took a long, deep breath and

forced herself to her feet, too, going inside herself and up to her room.

The room that faced the room Flint was in next door.

And if some secret part of her was tempted to stand in front of her curtained window to undress?

That particular bit of wickedness she *did* resist.

But Jessie the woman—not the mom, not the widow—couldn't keep from taking the idea of it to bed with her.

Along with the lingering effects of a kiss that had reminded her once again just how alive that woman in her was.

And could be again…

Chapter Eight

Guests began arriving at Kelsey and Coop's at four o'clock Sunday afternoon. The party itself was held in the backyard, where Jeannie and Jack Hunt were stationed with the kids. Kelsey and Coop were greeting people at the front door, then taking turns showing them around the house itself before depositing them in the kitchen where Jessie and Flint were to offer drinks before steering them to the yard.

It occurred to Jessie that what had begun as a pain in the neck—her sister manipulating things so that Jessie and Flint spent time alone together—was now something that she appreciated. Something she was glad their fake date hadn't done much to diminish. Because now that she secretly wanted to spend time alone with Flint, it didn't look at all odd when she got to because it was what her sister had assigned her to do.

And no amount of telling herself she should be avoiding it actually caused her to put up enough of a fight with Kelsey to accomplish that.

"What are you plans for tonight, when this party is over?" Flint asked her as they filled the ice bucket, made punch, opened wine and made sure there was beer and plenty of soda and iced tea in the refrigerator.

"Uh…my plans for tonight?" she repeated. "They're big ones— I'll help clean up from the party and/or put four kids to bed."

"After that. I was thinking that tonight might be a good time for me to take pictures of your sculptures. My website should be up and running this week and if I can get the photographs to my webmaster he can put them on the site so they'll be there for the launch. If you think you can manage it after you're finished being Super Mom…"

"And before I collapse," she said, still trying to rein in her happiness at the prospect of having time alone with him at the end of the evening.

"And before you collapse. Or you can collapse on the couch in your studio and just watch while I take the pictures."

Just watching Flint was never something she could deny herself and today, when he was dressed in a pair of gray slacks that just hinted at his well-shaped derriere and thick thighs, when he had on a crisp white shirt that accentuated his broad shoulders, any chance she had to watch him was not an offer she could even begin to make herself refuse. Plus she had the excuse of taking the first step in possibly being able to sell her sculptures to make money for the kids' college education.

"What do you say?" he asked when she had apparently been lost too long in those thoughts of tonight.

"If the party doesn't go too late," she agreed provisionally.

The doorbell rang just then, bringing their attention back to arriving guests.

Because the housewarming party included such a large contingent of the Fortune family and their close friends the Mendozas—who were also relatives by marriage in several instances—having Flint by her side provided Jessie with an opportunity to be reminded who everyone was.

"I think I met most of your family at the last party—"

"The one where you met me," Flint said with joking innuendo.

She rolled her eyes. "The one that welcomed Anthony into the family. But I met so many people then that there's no way I can remember who's who. Of course I know William and Lily, and Ross and Frannie and their families. But it would help if you could jog my memory about everyone else," she told Flint as they took their position at Kelsey's kitchen table, which gave them a clear view of the front door.

"There are a lot of us," Flint commiserated.

"And a lot of things that have gone on since William and Lily's wedding didn't happen in January. I know bits and pieces of it, but could you give me the gist of things so I don't make any insensitive faux pas?"

"Are you just looking for a way to get the scoop on the family soap operas?" he teased.

"No, really," Jessie insisted, meaning it. "Wasn't there

some kind of rift between your Uncle William and one
of his sons—"

"Drew."

"I'd hate to say something that would make anyone
uncomfortable. And if there's anything else…"

Flint just grinned at her, knowing she wasn't fishing
for gossip. Then he nodded in the direction of the front
door. "My cousins are all coming in now," he informed
her. "Those are William's kids—Drew, JR, Nicholas,
Darr and Jeremy—"

"I know Jeremy—he's one of the doctors at the clinic.
I saw him when I took Adam to the doctor a few weeks
ago for an ear infection. I also know that he used to live
in California, but he stayed in Red Rock when your
Uncle William went missing to try to help find him."

"Yep. And while he was here, he met Kirsten—that's
her beside him—and now they're engaged."

"That I knew, too. And I know JR—he's the rancher.
Kelsey helps with his horses, that's how she and Coop
met. And JR is married to Isabella Mendoza."

"Right. Moving on—that's my cousin Darr. He's a
local firefighter, and that's his wife, Bethany, and her
baby daughter, Randi. Then there's Nicholas—he's our
financial analyst. He moved to Red Rock in February.
That's his wife, Charlene, holding baby Matthew."

"Okay," Jessie said, trying to apply all the names and
details to memory once and for all. "But don't forget
to tell me about the problem between your uncle and
Drew," Jessie prompted.

"Drew is the vice president of Fortune Forecasting—"

"Which forecasts what?"

"They predict marketplace trends," Flint said. "But

Uncle William is the CEO. Everyone—including and especially Drew—was sure that when Uncle William was ready to retire, he would hand the reins of the business over to Drew, and that that would happen when Uncle William and Lily got married. But just before that, Uncle William dropped a bombshell on Drew—William decided that Drew's life was out of whack, that he was too much of a workaholic and neglected his personal life, that if he was left to his own devices, Drew would end up alone."

"And your uncle didn't want that for his son."

Flint pointed a long index finger at her to let her know she was right on the money. "So Uncle William said that until Drew found someone, got married and started to have a life outside of work, William wasn't budging from the CEO seat, which caused a lot of tension between them."

Jessie nodded in the direction of the group of people talking in the entryway. "Drew seems to be with someone," she observed.

"Deanna. His wife."

"His wife?"

Flint's expression showed his amusement. "It seems that my illustrious cousin hatched a plan of his own— Deanna was his marketing assistant and he tried to convince her to marry him just for show. But Uncle William's disappearance put that on hold and in the meantime, Drew discovered that Deanna was the real deal after all. They eloped to Las Vegas at the end of January."

"But your uncle was still missing then and since they've found him he hasn't remembered much of anything, so where has that left Drew?"

"Still vice president. Even though Uncle William isn't really in any shape to be the acting CEO, getting his mind back on track is the priority now. That's why Drew and Deanna are in from San Diego—they come in every chance they get to visit William."

"So the rift is just sort of in the shadows—William doesn't even remember it."

"But Drew is still sitting second chair when he thought he'd be in the first by now."

"So I won't make small talk with Drew by asking about his work—it's bound to be a sore subject."

"Probably for the best."

The front door opened yet again for another couple to join the party.

"That's Wendy—"

"She's so young," Jessie said.

"She's from the Atlanta branch of the Fortunes. They sent her here hoping she might get her head together, find some direction."

"And did she?"

"She started out working for the Fortune Foundation, which you probably know does the funding and the fund-raising for the clinic where Jeremy practices and a slew of other charities and good-deed organizations. But Wendy was…let's say, not suited to the office work. She's bubbly and full of energy and she just didn't fit into the environment at the Foundation. The family thought she might be happier in a more social atmosphere and asked the Mendozas to hire her at Red—that's where she met Marcos Mendoza, in February, and now they're engaged, too."

The first contingent of Fortune and Mendoza guests moved into the kitchen. Flint greeted them all warmly, and Jessie thought that the new connection he felt to them was clear. He also reacquainted family and family friends with Jessie, reminding them she was Kelsey's sister.

When small talk had been exchanged and everyone but Jessie and Flint moved on to the backyard, Jessie nodded in the direction of the front door once more. "I know that's Rafe Mendoza. He's the lawyer who helped with the legal stuff that went along with Coop finding Anthony…"

"And that's his wife, Melina. They were high school sweethearts who lost touch and rediscovered each other. I believe that happened about March. I know they were married recently in a small family ceremony."

"How nice that they found each other again," Jessie commented, thinking of her own high school relationship with Pete and how glad she was that they hadn't had any lost years.

And out of nowhere she suddenly had such a strong sense of her late husband that she couldn't help feeling that he was there with her, in spirit if not in body. It was somehow comforting and difficult at once, making her miss him, wish that he *was* there in body, and at the same time, feeling guilty again for being beside Flint—for being so glad to be there.

But the feelings were chased away when the former-high-school-sweethearts-turned-newlyweds joined Jessie and Flint in the kitchen then, just as friends of Kelsey, and friends of the Hunt family began arriving.

Then, as Rafe and Melina went outside and Kelsey took that group on the house tour, William and Lily arrived.

"Look at that," Jessie said when she and Flint were alone again. "Your uncle and Lily are just beaming."

Flint returned from a trip to the freezer to refill the ice bucket, setting it down before he glanced into the other room.

He chuckled slightly when he did. "You're right. I wonder what's up with them."

Coop was obviously aware that something was going on with the older couple, too, because Jessie saw his perplexed smile as she caught just enough of what he was saying in the distance to know he was questioning them about their joyful moods.

His answer was more laughter and the exchange of gleeful looks between Lily and William without getting an explanation. Instead, after William said something Jessie couldn't hear at all, she saw Coop apparently concede with a shrug before he said, "Sure, I'll take care of that. You're the last arrivals, so let me show you around first and then—"

"We can't wait!" Lily responded excitedly. "Show us the house later."

"Okay," Coop agreed.

When Kelsey brought their other guests from upstairs, there were too many voices for Jessie and Flint to be able to decipher what Coop told Jessie's sister. But after that everyone, including Cooper and Kelsey, came into the kitchen.

Coop and Kelsey pitched in to fill drink orders and then ushered everyone out to the backyard, telling Flint and Jessie as they did, "Uncle William needs a family audience. I don't know what's going on, but I promised that I'd get everyone's attention."

"He probably just wants to give a toast or something," Kelsey suggested.

But Kelsey hadn't been in the entryway to witness what Coop had, what Flint and Jessie had seen from the kitchen.

"Maybe," Coop allowed without conviction, "but let's go. I said I'd do it right away. You and Jessie, too, Flint," Coop added.

The backyard was brimming with guests and the children of guests to join Braden, Bethany, Adam and Ella. Once Coop, Kelsey, Jessie, Flint, William and Lily were outside on the deck, Cooper tapped a spoon on the side of a glass to call attention to the gathering.

He thanked everyone for coming, gave a general introduction of his uncle to those of Kelsey's friends who might not know him, and said that William had asked to say a few words. Then Coop picked Anthony up from the infant swing to hold on his hip as Coop, Kelsey, Flint and Jessie stepped off the deck and gathered in their own small semicircle on the grass below to face William Fortune.

Jessie hadn't met the older man before he'd been located in Haggerty and brought home to Red Rock. Since then he'd been in a daze, uncertain of himself, of everything and everyone around him. But the man who stood at the edge of the deck, facing the large crowd, was a much more commanding presence. He stood tall and straight, sure of himself.

"For those of you who may not know," he began, "our family has had some difficult months that began on New Year's Day when I was scheduled to be married to this wonderful woman—"

William held out his hand for Lily to take and brought her to stand beside him.

"Until just a few days ago, I couldn't explain what had happened to me or what had led up to it. Ultimately we all learned that I was in a car accident that left me not even knowing who I was. It took months for my family to locate me, to bring me home, and still when I looked into my Lily's face, when I looked at my own children, my own nieces, nephews, my own family and friends, they were all strangers to me. Some of the mystery has been uncovered in small pieces along the way—like who Anthony's mother was, that Coop is his father, that his mother was lost in a car accident of her own..." William paused as if out of respect for Anthony's late mother. "And then, on Tuesday when Lily and I were here, when I looked in on Anthony—"

William cast a fond glance at the baby.

"—the curtain that was hiding my memories began to lift. And since then it's been as if little by little, that curtain kept on rising until I finally recalled everything," he finished victoriously.

"It's true," Jeremy said to the mutterings of almost all of the Fortunes and the Mendozas and everyone else who was aware of the turmoil that the family had been in recently. Smiling broadly himself suddenly, he said, "Lily called me yesterday. I had a neurological evaluation done at the clinic, and if he isn't a hundred percent, he's at least ninety-nine."

"Well, don't leave us hanging any more than we already have been," Flint joked from beside Jessie. "What the hell happened to you?"

"That old girlfriend of yours, Coop—Lulu? Anthony's mother? She called me just as I was getting dressed for the wedding. She said she'd read about my engagement to Lily, about the wedding date. She'd tried to reach you, but couldn't—"

"Neither could the rest of us when we needed to know if he was Anthony's father," Drew contributed.

"I know, I know," Coop said. "I took the loner thing pretty far—traveling around, not keeping contact with anyone. But all that's changed," he added, rubbing Anthony's back, smiling at Kelsey.

"At first Lulu said she thought you might have been coming to the wedding," William went on. "I said you were, that you were in Red Rock. But that changed her tune, she seemed panicky, she said she didn't want to face you. She told me that she'd realized she was pregnant just after the two of you had broken up, that you'd already left Minnesota and that she hadn't been able to locate you. She'd had the baby—Anthony—but after that she'd lost her job. She'd become depressed, she just wasn't able to handle being a mother, and I can tell you that just from my one conversation with her, she was definitely troubled."

Jessie saw the dark frown that was clouding Coop's expression as his uncle went on.

"Lulu said that you'd told her that you didn't have any intention of ever marrying, of having children, and I think she was worried that you might refuse to take Anthony if he came to you through her. She said that you had talked about your family—me, Patrick, Ryan…"

William cast a caring glance at Lily when he said the name of his cousin, her late husband.

Then he went on. "Lulu said that the family here in Red Rock was the kind of family you'd wished for yourself, and she thought it was the kind you would wish for Anthony, too. So she wanted me to take him, to raise him if you wouldn't, to give him a home or at least find him one among us."

Jessie saw more emotions cross Coop's expression—guilt, regret, sadness—and watched her sister grasp his arm, offering support.

"Lulu was so upset on the phone," William continued from there. "She definitely didn't sound stable. I tried to calm her down, I told her to just come to the wedding, to bring Anthony, that I'd get her together with you, Coop, that everything would be all right. But she wouldn't listen. She insisted that I had to go to her and take the baby. I said my wedding was in barely an hour, but she wouldn't have it any other way, so I told her I'd see what I could do to get there."

"And that's what he tried to do," Lily announced. "That was where he was off to just before the wedding. He thought he could make it to Haggerty, where Lulu was staying. That he could either reason with the woman and persuade her to come back to Red Rock with him, or at least get Anthony and make it back for the wedding."

"But when I got to the motel where Lulu said she was staying, she was gone. I thought she'd either changed her mind about giving up the baby or that she might have done what I'd asked after all and come to Red Rock. So I headed back here, in a hurry to get to the wedding…"

William cast an apologetic glance at Lily. Jessie saw him squeeze Lily's hand before he continued with his account.

"But there's that curve in the road just outside of Haggerty…" William said. "I was driving fast, to get back for the wedding, and as I came around that curve there was a car coming toward me, over the line. I had to swerve to keep from crashing into it. I heard the screech of tires and a crash behind me, but I couldn't control my own car—I must have hit a bad patch in the road. I spun out and down the side of the embankment..." William shook his head. "And everything went black."

"It had to have been Lulu's car you nearly crashed into, that crashed when she swerved to miss hitting you, too," Ross said then. The car that they'd already learned Lulu had been driving, the accident that had killed her. "And because we know now that Anthony had been left on the church steps—"

"Maybe Lulu was worried that Uncle William wouldn't go to Haggerty to get Anthony after all," Coop put in. "She must have brought him to the church and then been on her way back to Haggerty—"

"When her path and Dad's crossed on that curve," Drew finished.

"I know she was terribly disturbed when I talked to her," William said. "She probably shouldn't have been driving. And I was rushing to get to my Lily..."

"It wasn't your fault," Jessie heard Lily say to William in a tone meant for him alone.

"We should all just be grateful that Anthony wasn't in either car, and that you came out okay, Uncle William," Flint insisted.

There was another somber moment when Jessie had no doubt that the woman who had died, Anthony's birth mother, was in all of their thoughts. But then Cooper seconded Flint's sentiments and set off a chain reaction of relief and gratitude from the rest of the family.

In the midst of that, William said in a booming voice that carried across the yard, "One more thing!"

Everyone quieted again.

"My darling Lily, who never doubted that something beyond my control had kept me from the first wedding, has again agreed to be my bride. And because we've waited long enough, we've set the date for Saturday— two weeks from yesterday!"

That truly broke the serious undertones. Laughter, clapping and cheers greeted that news as many of the Fortunes approached the deck to shake William's hand, to hug Lily, to congratulate the couple anew.

But as Jessie looked on, taking in the Fortunes' well-earned happiness, seeing all the contented couples, re-calling who was engaged to whom, and added to it now the announcement of yet another wedding so soon, a strong wave of melancholy overwhelmed her.

Then, compounding it, she heard her sister say, "Let's break open the champagne now, toast our new house, Uncle William getting his memory back and the wedding after all."

But just when Jessie wasn't sure she could participate, when she was tempted to slip away altogether before her own feelings put a damper on anything, Flint winked at her.

"Champagne sounds like our department," he said, drawing her into the warmth of a gaze that was for her alone and unwittingly giving her strength.

And that was when she knew that what was really going to get her through the next few hours of that party, of everyone else's happiness and celebration, was the simple thought that when it was over, she would have Flint Fortune all to herself.

Chapter Nine

The party went on until nearly ten o'clock Sunday evening as everyone but Jessie threw themselves into celebrating.

The general consensus was that William regaining his memory was the turnaround for the Fortune family after half a year of turmoil and strife.

But because that turmoil had also brought some good in the form of five different couples finding each other, of the new addition of Anthony to the family, and of Coop not only discovering he was a father, but of Coop and Flint also coming into the Fortune fold in a way they hadn't been before, the family was also grateful. And that gratitude, coupled with the relief that William was back to himself, put them in a festive mood.

When the party finally did begin to break up, Jessie's parents took her kids home to put them to bed and

Jessie stayed to help Kelsey, Coop and Flint clean up. With four of them working it didn't take too long and by eleven Kelsey and Coop said good-night, leaving Flint and Jessie in the kitchen.

"What do you say?" Flint asked then. "Think you can collapse on the couch in your studio while I take pictures or are you too tired for even that?"

The emotions that the evening had stirred in Jessie had zapped her energy and she *was* beat. But even so she couldn't bring herself to call it a night before having those few moments alone with him that she had been craving all evening.

"As long as I only have to collapse on the couch while you work, I think I can manage it," she told him.

He reached to the top of Kelsey's refrigerator and took down a small digital camera. "Then let's do it," he suggested, sounding far more lively than she felt.

Turning off the kitchen lights and closing the door behind them, they went into the now-quiet backyard, crossed to the gate in the side fence and headed for Jessie's studio.

She let them into that, turned on the lights at both ends of the open space and then went directly to the sofa where she kicked off the sandals that had been on her feet for too long today, and sat sideways on the couch so she could put her legs up.

"Aah…" she sighed as she settled in.

And before she knew what was happening, Flint took his first snapshot—of her.

"No, no, no, no, no—that wasn't our deal," she chastised. "No pictures of *me!*"

She'd made a pit stop in her sister's bathroom just a little while ago to be sure she didn't look too haggard.

The khaki slacks and the red scoop-necked T-shirt she'd worn to the party weren't excessively wrinkled, and the lace camisole she'd worn under the T-shirt still peeked pristinely above the neckline.

Her mascara and blush had held up, and so had the French twist she'd put her hair into, leaving her with only the need to fluff the curls that spewed from the top of it at her crown.

She'd borrowed Kelsey's new lip gloss because her own had disappeared, but regardless of the fact that she'd left the bathroom satisfied that she was still presentable, she hated having her picture taken and certainly didn't want it done now, unawares, by Flint.

And yet he snapped a second one despite her refusal.

"Don't make me come over there…" she said as if he were one of her kids.

It made him laugh. But he turned the camera away with an "Okay, okay" that sounded exactly like Braden did when he was being forced to stop his mischief.

Without having to contend with being photographed, Jessie restarted her relaxation process. She sank farther down on the sofa cushion, bent her legs at the knees and got comfortable.

"Oh, I'm glad that party is over," she said, realizing only after the fact that that probably wasn't something to admit to Flint.

But he was turning one of her sculptures this way and that to make sure he got the best angle and seemed to take the remark in stride. "Yeah, I didn't think you were having a great time. I'm just not sure why—it was a nice party."

"It was," Jessie agreed quickly.

"Not a fan of the Fortunes—because it did end up being more about our family than anything, didn't it?"

"No, it isn't that," she answered even quicker. "Your family has all been wonderful—so welcoming to Kelsey and the rest of us, friendly and sweet. We're all glad your uncle got his memory back, and Lily even extended a personal invitation to me, the kids and my parents to come to her and William's wedding."

She hadn't intended to end that in a tone of voice that hinted at being maudlin, but she had. And Flint must have heard it because he stopped mid-photograph to glance at her.

"And that offended you somehow?" he said, clearly trying to figure out what was going on with her.

"No," she said yet again. "That was nice, too. It's just that…"

Was this something to talk about with Flint of all people?

She didn't know. But she also didn't want him to think she had any bad feelings about his family, so she shrugged and said, "It's just me. Engagements, pending weddings, weddings—since Pete died they just bring me down a little."

"Oh, sure they do!" he said as if he'd had a revelation. "And that party—wow, pretty much everybody but you and I were either married, newly married or engaged. And then the big announcement of Uncle William and Lily's wedding? Of course that couldn't have been a barrel of laughs for you. Geez, Jessie, I'm sorry."

"Oh, no, there's nothing for you or anybody else to be sorry about. Life goes on. My own sister is one of the engaged, for crying out loud. It just kind of hit me—that happens sometimes."

And if it wasn't for you I wouldn't have been able to weather it as well as I did, she thought.

She didn't tell him that, though. It wasn't something she fully understood herself, and she definitely didn't want to admit that that had been the case.

Flint didn't say more either, concentrating on taking his pictures, and it struck her that he was at a loss for what else to say on the subject. But that was okay. It left her to merely watch him—one of the original enticements of letting him do this tonight.

And watch him she did, drinking in the sight of him, tall and lean, muscular, dexterous, his big hands wielding the camera, carefully altering the positions of her sculptures to get the exact shot he wanted of each piece.

He could do as right by a pair of slacks as he could by a pair of jeans, Jessie decided, but as she studied him she realized that she preferred him in the jeans. She liked the more casual look that didn't in any way mute his intense masculinity.

But the white shirt? That set off his dark coloring, the bittersweet chocolate tones of his carelessly disheveled hair, the espresso eyes, the healthy-looking, slightly sun-bronzed hue of his skin.

She thought that he must have shaved just before the party had started because his beard hadn't made much of a reappearance yet, leaving the lower half of his handsome face smooth and unshadowed. And after considering it, she still couldn't make the choice between liking him better scruffy or clean-shaven, and had to accept the fact that there just wasn't a way she *didn't* like the look of that face.

The time he spent photographing her sculptures passed before she knew it. "Okay, I think those will work," he said, setting his camera on the table near the door, then coming to the sofa.

Without asking permission, he bent over, clasped Jessie's knees to lift her legs, sat down and then lay them across his lap. Resting his arm atop them there, he turned to face her, stretched his other arm along the back of the couch cushions, and finally settled in to look intently at her.

"Now," he said as if the time had come for something. "Tell me about Pete."

The way he said that somehow touched her. Beyond the platitudes, she'd learned since her husband's death that people rarely knew what to say. And that most of them, even family, avoided talking outright about Pete, probably because they thought it was painful for her to be reminded of him. Remembering him, thinking about him, did bring its fair share of pain, but at the same time, she hated having her life with Pete be an untouchable subject.

And when it came to that subject with another man? Flint had opened that door himself and seemed to acknowledge and honor her history with Pete. It allowed her to claim him openly. It made her feel free to talk about him.

And tonight—even though it hadn't occurred to her before now—she realized that she *wanted* to talk about her lost husband. That after having the sense that his spirit was with her today, after enduring hours of a renewed feeling of loss in the face of so many other happy couples, he was on her mind right along with Flint.

"Pete and I were high school sweethearts—like Melina and Rafe Mendoza," Jessie said. "Only we didn't break up and then have to rediscover each other. Once we met, we stuck like glue."

"Did you meet at the beginning of high school?"

"No, Pete transferred in our senior year. But we did literally crash into each other walking into the building the first morning of senior year—he accidentally bumped me, I dropped my books, he helped me pick them up and that was it, like a movie," Jessie couldn't help smiling as she recalled the slapstick meeting.

"We were together from then on," she continued. "That first day made it seem like kismet because we somehow ended up in five out of six classes together. Not to mention lunch—Pete was an outgoing kind of guy and he just came over to the table where I was sitting with the whole group of my friends, made a joke that had us all laughing, then asked if the new kid could join us, and we even had lunch together. That was Pete—he was funny and a flirt right from the start, and... Well, I know people say it all the time, but being with each other came so easily, so comfortably, that it was as if we were meant for each other."

She didn't want to think about the fact that she felt much the same way with Flint. That sitting there, with her legs in his lap, seemed as natural as everything had with Pete.

"By the time we graduated neither of us wanted anything as much as to get married. So we made that our first goal—my engagement ring was my graduation gift, we set a date and—"

"College, or art school," he said pointedly, referring to their conversation the other night, "weren't high on your to-do list anyway, so you just got your life started. Even though you were both really young…"

"Right. But you know how it is, you feel like you're all grown up."

"I do know how it is," he said and she knew he was thinking about himself, about getting out on his own at that early age, too.

"Pete's dad was an electrician," Jesse went on. "He helped Pete get an apprentice position that didn't pay much, but gave him training and experience to go along with the night classes he took at a trade school. His dad also got me a job in the office of the construction company he worked for."

"Was this the same construction company you were both working for when…"

"Yes. Pete's dad had retired by then, so he wasn't working for them anymore, but Pete and I still were."

Flint nodded. "And the wedding?"

"We were married the week after we both turned nineteen."

"You both turned nineteen at the same time?"

"Our birthdays were three days apart."

"Wow, you really were two peas in a pod."

"Not completely, but we did have a lot in common. I told you, it was as if we were meant for each other."

"So you got married at nineteen…" Flint said to keep her going.

"And then we set Goal Number Two—we wanted to buy a house. That took us five years of saving on an apprentice electrician and an office clerk's salaries, but we celebrated our fifth anniversary moving in here."

The memory of that, of their first night in the house, of sleeping bags opened in front of the fireplace in the living room just so they could be there, the memory of ceremoniously throwing out the birth control pills and making love to christen the place, hoping to start their family that same night, brought a flood of tears to Jessie's eyes.

"You were happy," Flint said very, very quietly, apparently seeing how frantically she was fighting the tears and guessing that it wasn't only sadness that had brought them on.

"We were," she whispered.

Flint gave her a few moments, running a purely comforting hand up and down one of her shins, and amazing Jessie with the fact that she could sit there with him—a man she was attracted to in so many ways that made her feel guilty—and still talk about this, still feel the way she was feeling, share it all with him, and even be comforted by him.

Something that multifaceted was something she would have been able to do with Pete. And yet now she was doing it with Flint.

And it was very confusing.

It was also a phenomenon she didn't want to explore, so as soon as she gained control over the tears and kept them from falling, as soon as she could clear her throat and go on, she took a deep breath and jumped ahead. "A year later Ella was born—having a family was Goal Number Three. And once the babies started coming—" She laughed. "It seemed like boom, boom, boom, we had four of them."

Flint hesitated another moment. Then he said, "And it's been two years now, since the accident?"

She drew another deep breath and blew it out completely, realizing as she did that talking about this tonight had been beneficial. It had cleared the clouds that had gathered at the party this afternoon and left her feeling much better.

Better enough to be able to answer Flint more matter-of-factly. "Yes, two years," she repeated.

"And since then, have you dated?"

That really made her laugh, although wryly this time. "Uh, no," she answered. "Despite Kelsey's nudgings in that direction, dating is about the last thing I've thought about."

Why that made him smile, she didn't know.

Then he said, "What about before the first day of your senior year?"

"I had three boyfriends before Pete, but I was too young for them to be serious. I'd kissed other boys and gone through infatuations, crushes and the breakups and heartbreaks that went along with them. But for anything other than that, for anything real? Pete was *It*."

"And now here I am," he said, very quietly. And while he'd gone on rubbing her shin, there was something about his touch that wasn't solely comforting anymore. Something that made it more alluring and intimate.

"How do you feel about that?" he asked.

For a split second she thought he wanted to know how she felt about the way he was rubbing her leg.

Then she realized that he was asking how she felt about what was going on between them—about the kissing they'd done, about the fact that she was sitting with her legs in his lap now, letting him give her what had become a sensual massage.

"It's kind of mixing me up," she confessed, once more

marveling at the sense of freedom she felt to even say that to him.

"In a bad way?"

"There's a little guilt—like I'm being unfaithful."

"But?" he said the word she'd clearly left unspoken.

She sighed. "I know Pete is gone. Nothing will bring him back. Everyone tells me it's time to go on…"

But when it came to considering that in the form of another man, she'd honestly thought she wouldn't be able to do it. That no man would measure up to Pete or what she'd felt for him. That she would never be able to have with anyone else what she'd had with him. That no relationship would ever be as effortless. That she would never be able to relax, to let her guard down so completely.

And yet here she was, with Flint, and she couldn't seem to keep herself from doing just that…

"You do need to go on," Flint said then, adding his support of what everyone else in her life advised.

"Or maybe things just go on when they're ready, naturally," she said, more to herself, looking at him sitting beside her, more than she seemed able to resist no matter how confused she felt.

He smiled thoughtfully. "True enough. Life moves on and there's no stopping it."

Or him either, maybe, because he pulled her by the legs then to sit with her rear end right up against his thigh, bringing her close enough to look into her eyes.

"Seems like there are a lot of things that there's no stopping," he said just before he kissed her.

And it was the sweetest kiss. Soft and gentle, warm

and inviting and so, so tender. So full of compassion and caring. And promise...

Jessie pressed a palm to his chest but not to push him away. In fact, though it seemed odd to her, for the first time kissing him *didn't* make her feel guilty.

Had talking about Pete, being open with Flint about her late husband, freed her in that way, too?

Maybe. Because as her lips responded to Flint's, guilt was nowhere to be found.

One of his hands came up to the side of her face, stroking her cheek while his other arm went around her back, pulling her more closely to him.

Mouths opened by degrees until there was room enough for tongues to meet, to play, to tease and cavort.

Flint repositioned them both and Jessie's arms ended up around him. Her hands roamed over his broad shoulders and muscular back as he cradled her head against the increasing blitz of a kiss that had moved from sweet to spicy.

Deliciously spicy...

And away went all thoughts of other couples, of engagements and marriages and weddings-to-come. Away went even lingering thoughts of Pete, leaving just Jessie. Just Flint.

His hands were in her hair, cupped around the column of her neck, massaging her shoulders and upper arms, and then her back in a way that again made her nipples stand at attention within the built-in bra of her camisole.

She wondered if he could feel them against his chest, straining and screaming for some of what he was doing to her back, her shoulder blades.

It was impossible to feel him caressing other parts of her and not want that same caress on her aching breasts. She was nearly lying across his lap by then and she arched her spine, pressing just a bit more into him, tightening her own arms around him, just trying to find a little relief as mouths opened wide and the intensity of that kiss took another leap.

As if he were testing the waters, Flint found the hem of her shirts and slipped his hands underneath them, to just rest on the small of her back.

Warm, calloused, infinitely gentle—not even the tiniest hint of guilt came with a touch that felt so good Jessie's breath caught in her throat.

Up those hands went, splayed to her back, dragging her shirt with them and leaving cooler air to kiss her flesh in their wake.

She loosened her grip on Flint. She relaxed back ever so slightly, craving the feel of his hands everywhere…

But that craving was left to grow while he worked the tension out of her muscles as effectively as any masseur, as his tongue continue to flirt with hers, making her desires grow…

It seemed like an eternity, but it hardly took any time at all before she was putty in his hands, before all that was left in her were those desires, as one of his wondrous hands began a slow slide along the very bottom of her ribcage, coming to rest just below her left breast.

She took a deep breath, and Flint's mouth opened even wider over hers, taking that kiss into pure abandonment, almost making her forget that her nipples had turned to diamond-hard pebbles of need.

Almost, but not completely, and when that hand finally rose by slow, steady increments, when it finally closed around her bare breast, she couldn't keep a tiny moan from rumbling in her throat, or from insinuating herself that much more firmly into his grip.

She'd forgotten how good that could feel!

And it did feel mind-bogglingly good as his fingers pressed into her compliant flesh, as her nipple grew even harder within his palm, as he showed her just how adept he was with a mastery she'd never known before.

But just when she was beginning to get lost in the sensations, in all that was springing to life inside of her, just when she was beginning to think of where this could go from here and wanting it to, something completely unexpected popped into her mind.

Ella.

Her unhappy eldest daughter.

Jessie didn't know where it had come from, but there it was, that thought that was suddenly torture because it reminded her that while she might have been freed of her guilt over being attracted to Flint, she still wasn't altogether free. She still had four kids to consider. And how anything she did could affect them—particularly Ella, who didn't really care for Flint.

The groan that left her throat almost silently that time wasn't solely from pleasure. There was a measure of remorse to it, too, as the fact that she couldn't let this passionate play go on sank in.

She just couldn't...

But she wanted to so much the idea of ending it, of not kissing Flint, of not having his hands on her, of losing the wonders he was working at her breast, of not letting this all go where she so desperately yearned for it to go, was actually painful.

The kids, she reminded herself, for the first time since

she'd become a mother actually having to force herself not to lose sight of that, of them, when it would have been so easy to just give herself over to her own needs and desires at that moment.

Just another minute, she pleaded with herself, kissing him back with a new intensity, as if to get every drop of the last drink of water she might ever have. Digging her hands into his back and fighting the longing to stroke every inch of him…

The kids…

She drew her hands up and over Flint's shoulders to his chest, meaning to push him back, to send the message that this had to end. But instead she somehow discovered herself doing some massaging of her own to his pectorals.

But this did have to end, she told herself, even as her hand clasped over his at her breast, pressing him ever more firmly there for a moment before she brought that wet and wild kiss to a conclusion and muttered an almost incoherent, "I… We… Stop…"

It took a moment for Flint to register the message and even when he seemed to, his hand stayed within hers on her breast. Chuckling slightly, he said, "I don't know if you mean that…"

She didn't. But she had to anyway. And she knew she had to let him know that.

So she said, "I don't want to mean it. But I do," she assured in a tone of voice fraught with all of the unwillingness she felt.

But to prove she really couldn't let this go on, she finally took his hand away, hating the loss of it as her breast seemed to strain for more at the same time.

Flint took over from there, slipping out from under

her T-shirt to place that same hand along one side of her neck while he kissed the opposite side, nuzzling her and making it all the more difficult for her to stick to her guns.

But despite tipping her head to give him more access, despite closing her eyes again and losing another few minutes in the same warm sweetness of his mouth that had begun this, she whispered, "Really."

And then she tried not to hate it so much when he complied and stopped that, too.

"Okay," he agreed with a sigh of regret of his own.

Jessie opened her eyes as they both sat up straighter, as they leaned away from each other. But despite that separation, Flint ran his hands from her shoulders down her back to her hips before he took them away completely.

And that was when Jessie stood because to stay on that sofa with him was too much temptation.

Flint stood, too, and as he faced her he searched her eyes with his. "Are we okay?" he asked, apparently worried that he'd overstepped his bounds.

Jessie's laugh was wry. "Way, way too okay," she said.

His smile was so endearingly sexy that it almost defeated her resolves all by itself. He took her hand in his then, grabbed his camera, brought her with him to turn off the light across the room and then turned off the light at the door as he led her out, letting her close it behind them.

He kept hold of her hand to get her to walk him to the gate, too, releasing her only when they'd reached it.

Then, facing her again, he once more looked intently

down at her and asked with complete sincerity, "I didn't make tonight worse for you, did I?"

"No," Jessie said without hesitation because that couldn't have been farther from the truth. Then she confessed what she'd kept to herself earlier, "You got me through that party. And that…" she nodded in the direction of the garage studio but then didn't know what to say about what they'd just shared. She merely settled on, "No, you didn't make anything worse."

Except for churning up emotions in her that she wasn't sure how to handle.

He didn't look completely convinced but didn't push her for more. After another moment of studying her with an appreciation that only made her feel better still, he bent over and kissed her chastely before he said, "I don't want to, but I guess I better let you go."

Once again he brought his hand to rest tenderly against the side of her face. Then he took it away, kissed her forehead and went through the gate.

And Jessie had to swallow hard to keep from calling him back. To keep from saying she shouldn't have stopped what had been happening in the studio.

But she couldn't forget who she was, she told herself as she turned away from the fence and headed for her house. She couldn't forget how many responsibilities she had, how many people were depending on her to do what was right, to do what was best for them.

She couldn't forget how much could be at stake if she gave in to passion.

Even if every ounce of her being was crying out for her to do just that.

Chapter Ten

"Jessie... Are you still awake or did you just get up?"

Jeannie came into the kitchen at 3:00 a.m. and discovered her daughter sitting at the table.

"Still awake. I guess I have a little insomnia tonight," Jessie answered, though not in all honesty.

The truth was that she'd been having trouble sleeping since she and Flint had had their encounter on the sofa in her studio Sunday night. Since he'd left and she'd decided she should keep her distance from him because it was the only way she could be sure that things between them wouldn't get any more complicated than they already were.

And she *had* kept her distance from him. But now it was three o'clock on Wednesday morning, and while she knew that eventually—usually just as the sun was coming up—exhaustion would finally let her doze off for a few hours, she was tired to the bone.

Yet somehow still so stirred up thinking about the man, wanting to be with him, wanting *him,* that she couldn't merely lie down in her bed at a reasonable hour, close her eyes and fall asleep.

"I always wake up about now and come down for a glass of milk to help me get back to sleep," her mother said. "But you... Are you feeling all right?"

She knew what her mother was worrying about—for months after Pete's death Jessie hadn't been able to sleep. She'd wandered the house until all hours, frequently encountering her mother on Jeannie's nightly forays to the kitchen. And even when Jessie had finally felt as if she could close her eyes, she hadn't been able to face the bed she and Pete had shared. Instead she'd just slept on the couch downstairs.

She was sure that her mother was concerned that if she wasn't sleeping again, grief had made a return visit. So she said, "I'm fine. It isn't Pete."

"What is it, then?" Jeannie asked as she poured two small glasses full of milk.

"It's nothing," Jessie insisted.

Jeannie brought the two glasses with her to the table and sat across from Jessie, sliding one of the glasses over to her.

"Did you have a fight with Flint or something?" her mother inquired. "Because I've heard you up the last two nights, too. And we've all noticed that you don't seem to want to be anywhere near him since the party Sunday."

Living in the same house with her parents, living next door to her sister, didn't allow for much privacy.

"Why would Flint and I fight?" she said. "He took pictures of my rock sculptures after the party, and with the work finished on Kelsey's house there just hasn't been a reason for me to go over there as much. I thought I'd let her and Coop settle in without any more company."

Jessie could tell by the way her mother was looking at her that Jeannie wasn't buying that.

But still she felt compelled to add, "We're nothing but acquaintances, Flint and I—he's just Kelsey's soon-to-be brother-in-law. What could we possibly *fight* about?"

"I'm not blind, Jessie," Jeannie said.

What had her mother seen? Certainly Jeannie hadn't seen her peeking out the window in her room, secretly hoping for a glimpse of Flint next door in his. Despite the fact that she'd done a ridiculous amount of that in the last two days and nights, she'd always made sure that her bedroom door was closed.

But her mother might have seen Flint kiss her at the van after their rock hunt. Or on the back porch Saturday night. She might have seen Flint holding her hand as they'd walked to the gate Sunday night. And kissing her again then.

Everything had happened late enough for her kids to all be sound asleep. But maybe not her mother.

Jeannie smiled as if she knew the wheels of Jessie's mind were spinning and clarified for her. "I've seen you looking over at Kelsey's house every time you pass any window that faces that way. I saw you trip over the jungle gym pieces yesterday because instead of looking where you were going, you were craning your neck to spy on Coop and Flint digging that hole to plant the tree on the other side of the fence. I've seen your eyes glued to Flint *every* time he's been outside and you catch a glimpse of him. I saw you frozen in the middle of changing the girls' sheets this morning. I called your name three times before you stopped looking out their window at Flint up on Kelsey's roof—it was as if you were in some kind of trance or something. You like that man."

If that was all her mother had seen it wasn't so bad.

Jessie merely shrugged it off. "He's a nice guy. And he's not hard on the eyes."

Jeannie laughed and reiterated, "And you like him. The two of you have gravitated to each other at every meal we've had together, on game night, at the house-warming. Your face just lights up the minute he comes into a room. So why stay away from him? Especially if staying away from him is making you antsy and keeping you up nights?"

"It's just not that simple…"

"Well, sure it is."

"It was one thing when we were working on Kelsey's house—she needed the help and you'd signed on for doing more with the kids while I was there. But now that the house is finished, doing anything with Flint would take more time away from the kids. Plus Ella doesn't like him and—"

"Oh, stop!" Jeannie reprimanded. "Jessie, you're a good mother. You are. But you can't let those kids be all there is for you. You need other interests. Other outlets."

"That's why I do the stone sculptures."

"That's not enough," her mother insisted.

Jessie shrugged. "Pete's and my old friends don't call anymore now that I'm not part of a couple—and it *would* be awful to see them and be alone. My old girlfriends are all married, so whenever I'm with them it always ends up a pity party with all of them feeling sorry for me and saying they don't know how I do without Pete—"

"But now there's someone right next door who you like being with," Jeannie interrupted.

"Even if that were the case, bringing a man—especially a man like Flint who isn't interested in commitment—into the kids' lives right now is too much, too soon. It couldn't be good for them," Jessie said softly.

"It's not too much or too soon," Jeannie refuted. "But I'm not even talking about bringing a man into their lives," she repeated. "I'm just saying that there's nothing wrong with—while Flint is here—the two of you spending a little time together. He's someone your own age who makes you laugh. You just seem to enjoy each other's company. So why not ask him to take a walk, or have coffee, or go out to dinner with him again?"

Because things between us have already gone so far beyond that...

That was the answer to her mother's question, but that was the last thing Jessie was going to say to her mother.

Instead she said, "I just don't think it's a good idea."

"Taking a walk, going out to a dinner—those wouldn't even involve the kids. And your dad and I don't mind babysitting. That's part of why we're here."

"To raise my kids while I run around with men?" Jessie joked.

Jeannie laughed, shaking her head as if she thought Jessie were hopeless. But still she said, "We're here to help, and I think it helps *you* to get out a little. It isn't good for you—or for the kids—to put all you've got into them and their lives, and nothing into your own, Jess. You can't sacrifice *everything* for the kids. You can't. I know that seems like the way to go now—"

"And the easiest and safest thing for us all."

"But it isn't," her mother said firmly. "There has to be something outside of the housework and the laundry and the grocery shopping and taking care of the kids, something that's only for you, that recharges you—"

"I don't want to go to your quilting club, Mom."

"But *I* have my quilting club. And my once-a-month poker with the girls, and my book group—they all give me time to just be me. When I come back from those visits, I'm a new woman. And unless I'm mistaken, every time you come back from being with Flint, you're a new woman, too. So I say, don't fight it. He's not going to be here forever. But while he is, where's the harm in seeing him? Especially when *not* seeing him seems to keep you up nights?"

Jessie was afraid Jeannie was beginning to understand—too much.

"It's all just weird," Jessie confessed to keep whatever containment she could on what her mother was thinking. "For some reason I'm really comfortable with him. I have an easier time talking to him than I thought I'd ever have talking to a man who isn't Pete, an easier time being with him…" *Even in ways that I wish weren't happening so easily.* "But because he *isn't* Pete, I feel guilty. And taking time away from the kids on top of it… I don't know. I guess it's just a dilemma that's keeping me up nights right now."

"It's only a dilemma if you make it one. If you stop fighting what you want, the dilemma is gone," Jeannie said conclusively as she took her now-empty glass to the sink and left Jessie's untouched one in front of her. "Flint doesn't live here. He'll be gone before you know it. And if I were you, I'd make the best of it while you can."

Jessie couldn't suppress a grin when she thought that her mother had no idea what she was giving her permission for.

But what she said was, "That's part of the problem."

"Maybe," Jeannie allowed. "Or maybe that's exactly the right setup for you to get your feet wet with a man again."

Oh, how she would have liked to do that!

But it just wasn't as simple as her mother thought it was.

Not when Jessie imagined the day Flint would pack up and leave his brother's house and go on his merry way.

Without a backward glance.

Without her.

Leaving her with what she was very much afraid might be another great big sense of loss to deal with all over again.

And the thought of that scared her so much, that after breakfast later that morning, when Kelsey came next door to invite Jessie, the kids, Jeannie and Jack to dinner that evening at her house, and also mentioned that Coop and Flint would be working on the yard all day, Jessie couldn't make herself heed her mother's advice.

Instead she made the impromptu decision that she and the kids would be going rock hunting and having their usual cookout in the woods.

Jeannie didn't give away the fact that that decision had happened on the spot and went along with Jessie's ruse that rock hunting had been preplanned. But Jeannie did give Jessie a sad sort of look and shake her head at her when no one else could see.

It didn't matter. The thought of Flint being within her sight for the entire day to come, the thought of having another meal with him while still trying to maintain some distance, some reserve, some detachment, was too much to endure.

So she rounded up her kids and essentially ran like a rabbit to keep herself away from Flint—and the temptation she was too afraid to give in to.

Chapter Eleven

Sleepless nights made for extra time to get things done, so after a long day of rock hunting with Ella, Braden, Bethany and Adam, driving home and getting all four kids bathed and to bed, Jessie even managed to shower herself, shampoo her hair, unload the van and get all the rocks washed.

She'd just finished that when there was a knock on her studio door.

It was after ten o'clock and she didn't have to look to know that it was Flint who was standing outside of that door.

She willed him to go away, but then she heard his deep voice say ever so softly, "It's me, Jess," and she knew that wasn't going to happen.

She was aware that he could see the lights and would know that no one else would be using the studio at that time of night. So she didn't have a choice but to open that door to him.

And nearly wilt at that first close-up glimpse of him in days.

Tall and lean and muscular. His hair shiny clean and carelessly disheveled. His face clean-shaven and so handsome that it made her just want to stare at him for hours. Wearing a pair of low-slung jeans and a black T-shirt that hugged every inch of that sculpted body. And looking at her with those coffee-colored eyes that seemed to convey confusion and hopefulness at once.

How was she supposed to resist all that?

All that and his holding up a bottle of wine when he said, "I have news you're gonna want to hear and something to celebrate it with. Can I come in?"

If only she could say no.

"Sure, come in," she answered, stepping aside and working like mad to make it appear as if she was as aloof as she wished she truly were.

Certainly how she was dressed didn't give her away, though, and now she wished she'd done more with herself after her shower. But she hadn't thought she'd be seeing anyone else tonight and with Texas temperatures rising as the month of June progressed, she was in her bare feet and had only put on a simple, knit sundress cut like a tank top to fall in an A-line to a hem that barely reached her knees.

Plus, the only thing she was wearing underneath it was a pair of panties. And while there was nothing revealing or indecent about the black-and-white polka dot dress that had a very minor built-in bra, she still felt a little too uncontained. Especially when her nipples tightened up the minute she laid eyes on Flint.

Hoping it seemed casual, she crossed her arms over her chest, clasping each upper arm with the opposite hand, and pivoted on her heels to allow him into the studio.

"I wasn't expecting company," she said self-consciously, thinking, too, about her hair. Left with only a brushing after it had dried, it always formed waves that tonight she'd clipped back—again for the sake of cooling off. A few stray strands had escaped the clip to fall around her face and she wondered if she looked a mess because of it.

"You might not have been expecting company, but you look good enough to go to a party," Flint said with enough appreciation to be convincing. Especially when his dark eyes seemed glued to her even as he came in and closed the door behind them.

His compliment helped remove some of her concerns about her appearance, but the way he was looking at her was somewhat of a turn-on, and Jessie began to worry that the heat in her cheeks was going to become a full-fledged blush.

Then he grinned, held up the wine bottle again and said, "I have more than a dozen gift shops that want to buy your sculptures and three galleries open to display them for sale."

And shock replaced some of her discomfort. And some of the turn-on that had come with the purely primal awareness she seemed to have of him.

"You have twelve shops and three galleries interested just since Sunday?" she asked.

"Just since Sunday," he answered smugly. "I told you this stuff is salable."

"And you came to gloat?" she goaded.

"I came to celebrate. And to find out if something is wrong because I haven't seen you in three days."

Maybe a glass of wine would help calm her nerves.

Jessie went into the kitchen section in search of a corkscrew and two glasses.

"Nothing's wrong," she said along the way, glad she didn't have to look him in the eye when she did. "I just felt like I'd neglected the kids and put too much burden on my parents while I helped out with Kelsey and Coop's house, so I wanted to give the kids some concentrated attention and give my folks a break."

"Ah, that makes sense," he said as if he didn't doubt her word.

That went a long way in preserving the illusion she wanted to maintain, too—that she could kiss him—and more—on Sunday night, and take it so in stride that she hadn't given it another thought. The illusion that hid the fact that she had been nearly sleepless for the last three nights and plagued day and night with wanting more of that kissing—and even more than that…

With wanting *him*.

Instead, she could be breezy, as if Sunday night hadn't been completely out of character for her and knocked her for a loop.

"And now we can talk money," Flint said as he joined her at the kitchen counter, took the corkscrew she'd just located and opened the wine.

"Right…money," she repeated.

Pouring the wine, he said, "I purposely didn't discuss price with you before because I knew you'd undervalue your work."

He went on to tell her how much he was asking for

her sculptures and Jessie knew her shock had to show in her expression.

"Are you kidding?" she said.

"And that's for the small pieces that I offered to the gift shops. The bigger ones that I presented to the galleries will go for much more."

Jessie didn't think there was any color left in her face after he told her exactly how much more he was talking about.

"For rocks that I found in the woods?" she said in astonishment.

"It isn't the rocks themselves that we're selling. It's the artistry in the way you put them together."

"I can't believe it…"

Flint laughed. "Maybe we better sit down—you look like you need to."

Jessie was still doing math in her head while he led her to the sofa where they both sat in the center of it.

"This will help so much," she muttered as figures began to form.

"Good. I'm glad. Now tell me the truth—were the kids and your parents the *only* reasons I haven't gotten to see you yet this week?"

Oh. So she hadn't been off the hook on that score after all.

"You don't think those are reasons enough?" she countered because he'd again taken her by surprise and she was at a loss for an answer.

"Let's just say that kids and parents don't seem like reasons enough to me."

Jessie sipped the wine. "Maybe that's because you live a different life than I do—the life of a childless bachelor who doesn't have too much contact with your own parents."

He laughed, took a drink of his own wine, then said, "*Childless bachelor*—you do not make that sound like something anyone should want to be."

"You're not married—that makes you a bachelor. And you don't have any kids, so you *are* childless."

"But both of those things are just simple facts, not things I've been sentenced to for some kind of crimes I've committed."

The perplexed creases in his brow made her smile. She also thought that this line of conversation gave her another way to escape talking about why she'd kept her distance. And along with that she might also get the answers to some of the other questions she had about Flint. And his past.

"Why *are* you unmarried and childless?" she said with some challenge to her tone.

He laughed again. "I told you I was married once, years ago, but not for long enough to have kids."

Jessie shrugged as she took another sip of wine, then tucked her feet to one side and behind her so she ended up facing Flint, resting her arm on the top of the sofa cushions.

"How many years ago were you married?" she asked then.

"We were both twenty-two—that was seventeen years ago. Her name was Myra."

"How long *did* it last?" Jessie probed because as he drank his own wine he showed no signs that he was reluctant to talk about this.

"Seven and a half months."

"You weren't even married for a year?"

"Maybe that's what happens when you don't put any thought into it."

"You got married without putting any thought into it?"

"In Vegas. It was Myra's suggestion that rather than ending our fourth date, we get in the car and drive there for the weekend."

"You got *married* after just *four* dates?"

"We didn't go to Vegas to get married, we went to make a long weekend of the date. But once we got there, we did a lot of drinking, Myra said wouldn't it be funny if we just got married and—" He grimaced at the expression on her face. "I know how bad that sounds. It was stupid, believe me. But I was young and she was…" He shrugged. "The whole thing with Myra was a burn hot, burn fast, burn out kind of thing," he said. "That's what happens when it's purely physical."

"Purely physical?" she repeated, knowing she'd done too much of that but suddenly feeling some insecurity about the fact that Pete had been her one and only, about Flint not merely having had more than a single other partner, but also having been with someone with whom things had been so hot that he'd been swept all the way into an impromptu marriage.

"Myra was…intense," Flint continued. "In everything. In everything she liked, everything she disliked. In everything she said and did. In every emotion she had, including, especially and most of all, anger."

"Really."

"Actually, Myra was not just angry, she got enraged. At the drop of a hat. Anything she saw as a slight, or even imagined was a slight, meant a screaming match. Somebody talking in a movie theater—Myra would be the one to stand up and make a scene about it. Myra was..."

"Irresistible to you?" Jessie asked, not understanding how what he was describing had had any appeal to him.

"She was like riding the most extreme amusement park ride. I..." He shrugged again. "I just couldn't *not* do it. But once I had? Once the thrill was over? Disaster."

"In what way, besides her tantrums?"

"Well, strange as it may seem, insane sex is not enough to build a relationship on," he said facetiously. "And for Myra, insane sex was not even something she wanted to have monogamously. I came home unexpectedly one day and found her in the shower with another man."

"Oooh," Jessie said sympathetically.

"Uh-huh. And yet somehow, to Myra, I was in the wrong for coming home unexpectedly. So she had no qualms about taking every penny she could get her hands on, every meager possession of any worth that I owned, and consequently, every drop of pride I had, when she took off with her lover. In my car."

"Oh dear." Jessie merely muttered because she wasn't sure what to say to that revelation.

"So between Myra and everything I saw with my mother, I'd say there are worse things than being a bachelor."

"I guess it is good that you didn't have kids to get caught up in that," Jessie observed.

"What did I tell you?" he finished as if he'd been vindicated. "Now, back to what got me into this—how come you've made yourself scarce this week?"

Did he have to be so persistent?

Jessie finished her wine and set the glass on the end table, realizing that her tension over this had been helped somewhat by the liquor. It hadn't, however, given her another way out.

Before she could answer his question, though, Flint said, "It was Sunday night, wasn't it? Too much? Did I scare you?"

Jessie grimaced and shook her head. "That's kind of the problem," she said quietly.

"That I *didn't* scare you?" he asked, sounding confused.

"Sort of…"

He leaned far forward and around her to put his now-empty wineglass on the end table with hers. As he straightened up he drew his hand from her hip along the side of her thigh, to perch on her knee, leaving a ribbon of something glittery along the way.

She tried to ignore it but that was difficult when that glittery sensation seemed to scatter all through her.

"Why would my *not* scaring you be a problem?" he asked. But then, again before she had found an explanation, light seemed to dawn in him. "Oh, I know. You're feeling guilty about this—" he waggled a finger from her knee to make a motion between them. But he didn't remove his hand, instead he squeezed her knee when the waggle was over.

"Did you think," he said then, "that if you stayed away, went back to the status quo, there wouldn't be anything to be mixed up or feel guilty about? An out-of-sight-out-of-mind deal?"

"Pretty much," she admitted.

"Did it work?"

Jessie whispered, "No."

He leaned just slightly forward again and confided in return, "Well, because I couldn't get you out of my mind, I'm sure glad."

It didn't help anything to know that. In fact, as she looked into his eyes she thought she saw a vulnerability in them that hadn't been there when he'd been talking about his ex-wife. That quelled her fears that she couldn't compete with the other woman, the other *women* he might have known. But it also made that internal glitter sparkle all the brighter and caused goose bumps to erupt along the surface of her skin, making that element impossible to ignore.

Then he straightened away from her, raised his eyebrows at her again, loosened his grip on her knee and said, "Unless you'd rather I get out of here, leave you alone and let you keep working on it…"

She knew that if she said the word that was exactly what he would do. Leave. Leave her alone. That that would be the end.

But suddenly all the things her mother had said about getting her feet wet with a man again, about making the most of the time she had with Flint—knowing full well that there wasn't any forever in it—rang in her ears.

That, and the fact that she could no more have made herself tell him to leave right at that moment than she could have sprouted wings and flown made her decision for her.

"No, I don't want you to go," she admitted.

"Because now I don't mix you up?"

"You're still mixing me up pretty much."

"But?"

"My mom said it was okay," she joked.

That made him laugh. "Thank you, Jeannie," he said as if her mother were there with them.

Then the humor seemed to dissipate and he studied her face as if he needed a moment to drink in the sight of her all over again.

"I've missed you," he told her quietly.

It had felt like that to her, too, but she didn't want to admit it.

Then before she needed to, Flint put his other hand on the side of her face, tipped it upward and touched his lips to hers.

She couldn't explain it, but there was something meaningful in that kiss. Something that reconnected them after those three interminable days apart. And being with him wasn't only easy—the way she'd told her mother it was—this was more than easy, it felt as natural, as right as if it were fated.

And oh, but it was a kiss that Jessie had been starving for!

So when Flint's lips parted, hers did, too. When his tongue came to greet hers, it was a greeting she welcomed and eagerly answered. And when his free arm pulled her closer, her arms went around him and she did her part in bringing them together in order for her taut nipples to press to his chest.

He wasn't Pete. And yet Jessie had a sense of coming home that she also couldn't fathom. But there it was and she was very aware of fitting within the circle of Flint's arm, fitting against his big body, as perfectly as if she were made to be there.

His mouth opened wider over hers, deepening that kiss and injecting another level of intimacy into it as his tongue toyed more seriously with hers, as his hand at her knee began a steady climb.

When he encountered the hem of her dress she expected him to go underneath it. But instead he jumped over it and used that hand to release the clip that held her hair, to run his fingers through the waves.

It was reflex that brought one of Jessie's hands around to his chest then, mimicking what she wanted of him without any forethought, realizing what she was doing only when her hand stroked his chest.

But maybe Flint took it as a clue because he drew his hand from her hair and let it glide down the column of her neck to rest on her shoulder, to rub and knead and massage that.

Her breasts were straining against him, crying out for his attention, for that touch that she'd regretted robbing herself of for the last three days.

Maybe it was thinking about that frustration, that unquenched yearning that sent her hand from his chest to return to his back where she delicately dug her fingers into that T-shirt that hugged his body more closely than she ever could.

But then it occurred to her that she didn't have to mind the rules. That she could merely slip her hands underneath it.

Which was what she did—inching, massaging a path down the ever-narrowing vee of his back to pull the T-shirt from the confines of his jeans and snake her way underneath it just as she'd imagined, just as she wanted him to do with her dress…

Warm satin-over-steel—that was what his skin felt like. Honed muscles, tight tendons, sinews all rolled and rippled beneath her touch as he did some massages of his own—of her back, too, of her shoulder still, then of her upper arm.

And all while his mouth went on tasting hers, plundering and playing and building an ever-growing hunger in her that made her wriggle just a little for want of more.

It might have been that tiny wriggle. Or it might have been the diamond-hard crests of her breasts poking through her dress that relayed the message, but after one last pulse of her arm, his hand went to her ribcage where it paused a moment before he brought it the rest of the way around front.

And again there was a perfect fit as her breast nestled within his palm, offering just enough for his adept fingers to grasp and mold and work like warm clay.

But as with his shirt, what had seemed like too little covering for her when he'd first arrived, seemed like a brick wall between them now, and she craved the feel of his bare hand on her naked flesh, too.

Except that in thinking that it also occurred to her that there wasn't much to the dress. And she had next to nothing on under it. For him to get to her meant that she would be practically nude. And if that happened...

If that happened there would be no turning back and she knew it. So she knew she had to be sure before she relayed any more messages.

But she was sure, she realized when no alarms sounded in her brain to stop her. When it took an act of will to recall what had kept her from this on Sunday night.

Because what had kept her from this on Sunday night had been the thought of Ella, of her kids. And tonight it came to her that this wasn't about her kids. This wasn't about her being a mother at all. That the same way she'd longed for Flint for the last three days, the same way she'd dreamed of him, thought about him separate from anything that had had to do with anyone else, this was about Flint alone. And her. And wanting him. Wanting this. Here and now and no matter what kind of limits there were on what was to come.

This was just for her.

A bold thrust of her tongue exerted her newfound sense of herself before she tore her mouth from his long enough to pull off his shirt, wanting him to know that she was in this for real tonight.

"Jessie…" he said in a cautionary tone.

It just made her grin. "Flint," she countered brazenly.

"There's a point of no return…" he warned.

"And I'm already past it," she informed, making him laugh.

Still, he said, "Seriously?"

But her only answer was to take his mouth with hers and unfasten the button on the waistband of his jeans.

A low, guttural sound rumbled from his throat, and Jessie somehow knew that was yet another warning to her that he was going to take her up on this if she didn't back out now.

But she wanted it too much, she wanted *him* too much, and she didn't have any intention of leaving either of them in the state she'd left them in on Sunday.

And when she sent a coy tongue to convey that, it was like pushing the On button in Flint.

His mouth, his tongue went wild and unleashed. His hand didn't hesitate to slide under her skirt, to pull it all the way up with him when he rediscovered her breast without the barrier of clothes. And when he retook her breast it was in a deliciously unyielding grasp, squeezing, kneading, proving to her that he was capable of an artistry all his own.

But it wasn't only his hand she wanted there. And it wasn't the only part of her body that cried out for his touch.

Her hands were on his bulging biceps and she moved them both to his pectorals now, spending only a moment there before she began a descent that trailed down his rock-hard abdomen to find the zipper of his jeans.

And the long hard proof of just how much he wanted her.

So much that it was a little daunting. But so, so exciting, too, that she couldn't resist slipping just one hand inside to that hot, hard shaft.

The moan that came from him then was pure pleasure. Her dress came up and over and off in one fast swipe, leaving her in nothing but her panties when he laid her back onto the sofa, when he made quick work of shedding the rest of his clothes as if he needed to break free of chains.

And if what she'd found moments earlier with her hand had been impressive, it was nothing compared to the sight of him in all his magnificent, masculine glory.

He joined her on the couch then, straddling her calves to remove her panties before he laid down with her, partially beside her, partially over her.

One wondrous hand went with his mouth to her breasts, savoring, devouring, reveling in them while tongue and teeth set off a whole wealth of new desires in her.

Desires that raised one of her legs over his as her hands delved into his hair to hold him to the mounting needs he was building within her.

Needs that only grew more demanding when his hand went from her breast, down her belly, to slip between her legs as he drew her breast fully into the wet velvet of his mouth.

It was Jessie's turn to moan—a soft, breathy sound as he found even more ways to please and arouse her. Almost too many ways because she was rapidly losing control.

Again she reached for him, wanting nothing more than to have him inside of her.

But just when that was all she could think about, he slid away, out of her grip.

Protection...

Luckily he'd remembered what she'd been too enraptured to even think about. And just as luckily he was quick about applying it before he was there again, with her, over her, her legs straddling his hips now.

His hands were on either side of her head and he dropped enough to kiss her again, a kiss that was so much more than merely that as he lowered his hips to hers and eased himself inside of her as smoothly as if he'd been fashioned for that purpose alone.

And it felt so, so good that her breath caught in her throat as he began to move—slowly at first, easing in and out, teaching her body the feel of him, the way to embrace him, to close around him and accept him.

Then he picked up speed and with measured strokes carried her along, taught her the rhythm, the beat, the motion that best met and matched him.

Faster still, powerful thighs propelled him, pushed

him and drew him away again, as hers curled around him and held on, moving with him, holding him tight.

Even faster yet, he came into her and out again, taking her closer and closer to a peak that seemed almost unattainable until she actually did reach it, until he took her all the way there and set loose in her something so incredibly glorious that she could only cling to him, arching her spine off the sofa cushions, pulling him to her until she felt him achieve that same peak.

He plunged so deeply into her that she found a second, even greater height of pleasure, of ecstasy that picked her up and let her ride that additional crest all the way through his, finally, finally leaving them both satiated and spent at once.

Collapsing with bodies melded together, arms and legs entwined, Flint's face was turned into the side of hers while they both caught their breath.

Then he kissed her temple and said, "Maybe you should have warned me that under the surface you have a little bit of a wild streak waiting to come out."

Jessie couldn't help smiling at the thought that she'd managed to amaze him. Even just a little.

"Too much for you?" she teased.

His laugh was ragged and sexy. "I don't know. I might need another taste to tell."

"Really?"

She hadn't meant that to sound so hopeful but it made him laugh again. "Please don't tell me that surprises you."

It had. She just wasn't too sure why. Except maybe that because she hadn't thought beyond this once she didn't have a concept of anything more. Anything like Flint wanting more.

And it was such a nice thought…

He rolled to lie beside her then, although at least half of him was still molded to her and his thigh and arm were blissful weights keeping her close.

"Give me about half an hour's rest," he requested, placing a second kiss to her temple, his voice slow and thick enough to let her know he was drifting off even as he spoke.

Jessie merely smiled and closed her own eyes as three nights of sleeplessness caught up with her, too.

And as she drifted off herself there was just a moment when she wondered why it was that falling asleep in his arms felt like the one place she was meant to be.

But she told herself it was just an illusion of exhaustion and merely let herself have that feeling the same way she'd let herself have Flint.

Knowing it was only for now.

Chapter Twelve

Flint counted the eight days—and nights—that followed in Jessie's studio as his best. With his Uncle William's wedding ten days away, even before that night, he'd decided to stay in Red Rock until after the wedding. And even before that night, Jessie had had more to do with that decision than anything else.

But never had he expected that time to pass the way it did.

Days were spent much as they had been prior to that night—he went on helping his brother by lending a hand painting the outside of Coop's house and building a shed in the backyard—and he did some of his own work using his up-and-running website and getting the feel for how that was going to affect his business.

During the days, he saw Jessie here and there, and they had another rock-hunting outing with the kids plus a field trip with them to San Antonio for shopping, an animated movie and dinner. There was also a Fortune family picnic that Jessie and her family were included in, and so he got to have that day with her as well.

But the nights?

Flint lived for those.

After that first one in the studio, after they'd left it just before dawn to go their separate ways so no one would know they hadn't been in their respective beds as usual, they'd let everyone know that Flint had found buyers for Jessie's sculptures. From then on that gave them the excuse of meeting in the studio each and every night after the kids were asleep.

It wasn't a lie that they were working together to come up with a logo for Jessie, that they were attaching the printed logos to the sculptures, that they were organizing and packaging the sculptures and getting them ready for shipment. They did use the first hour or two of those nights doing just that.

But when that work was finished?

The remaining hours of each and every one of those nights ended up being spent the way Wednesday night had been spent—except that they made love not only on the sofa but in the bed, on the floor, on the table and countertop, in a chair, in the shower, almost everywhere they happened to be when keeping their hands to themselves suddenly became too much to bear.

But when William and Lily's wedding was a mere two days away, when the subject of Flint going home began to come up again and again with everyone except Jessie, Flint suddenly found himself in one hell of a funk.

He tried to tell himself that it was a result of how

nice it was to finally feel a part of the Fortune family. That that made facing going back to Denver, to the way things had been before less than appealing. He tried to tell himself that the reason he wasn't looking forward to leaving was that it was nice to have his cousins, his uncle, his brothers and sister nearby, to see them whenever he wanted, to have them drop in, to have impromptu lunches with them, with the Mendozas, at Red.

And it all made sense. The new connection he'd made with his family, with the Mendozas, with the Red Rock community *was* nice, so the thought of separating himself from it and going back to Denver where he had busy friends and acquaintances but no one close understandably didn't seem like such a good thing now.

But in spite of all that? Underneath it? He knew that the bigger reason he didn't want to leave Red Rock was Jessie.

And as he pounded shingles onto the roof of his brother's new shed, thinking about his uncle's wedding the day after tomorrow, about how there was no reason for him not to be on his way the day after that, the funk weighed heavily on him.

Never in his life had there been anything he didn't want to do as much as he didn't want to turn his back on Jessie and walk away.

Never in his life had there been a woman he felt about the way he felt about Jessie.

There had been plenty of women in his life, and yet there was no question that he hadn't just plain *needed* a single one of those women like he needed Jessie.

And not even the possibility of a long-distance relationship, of making sure he came through Red Rock a whole lot more often, helped.

He wanted every day, every night to be the way they were now. He wanted to know that every day was going to end with the two of them together.

He just didn't know how that fit with the fact that he was about as anti-marriage as any man could be. That after watching his mother run through too many men, after his own ugly lesson in the perils of marriage, he honestly believed it was not only a bad course to take, but also the worst course to take.

If Jessie were anyone else, the most he would suggest was that they try living together. But there were two ways in which Jessie wasn't *anyone* else. First of all, she had four kids and parents who already lived with her. That was not a situation open to a just-living-together scenario.

Second of all—and even more importantly—Jessie wasn't merely *anyone else* to him. And as unbelievable as it was, he wanted her to be a part of his life, of his future, in the most unbreakable way he could have. Which translated into marriage.

Which he didn't believe in.

He hit a nail so hard that it bent in half rather than going through the shingle.

Marriage.

He'd sworn he would never make that mistake again.

But the thought of Jessie and marriage?

Regardless of what he'd thought of the institution before, when he put it together in his mind with Jessie, it somehow didn't hit the same sour note.

Certainly she wasn't Myra, he acknowledged. Yes, the physical attraction to Jessie was every bit as intense.

But there was so much more to her than there had ever been to his ex-wife.

He admired Jessie. He respected her values. Those were not things he could ever have said about Myra.

Jessie was strong and resilient, loyal, trustworthy, reliable, dependable. There was nothing fly-by-night about her, nothing unprincipled or unscrupulous—like Myra. Like his mother, come to think of it.

And Jessie had even more qualities than the ones that reassured him that she wouldn't end up stealing him blind and running off with another man or dumping him for someone down the road who seemed like a better ticket.

Jessie was fun and funny and loving and cute and sexy and caring and sweet and smart and talented and interesting. She was everything he'd ever found in any other woman, only she was all of it rolled into one.

She was everything to him.

That realization stopped his arm in midair, midhammer, when it struck him.

Jessie was everything to him.

It was true. Shockingly, surprisingly, stunningly true.

So Jessie and marriage? That was something that he could not only suddenly see as a possibility, but it was also something he discovered when he actually considered it, that he wanted.

He *wanted* to marry Jessie...

And have every day for the rest of his life end with the two of them together...

"Hi, Fwint!"

The sound of Adam's voice made Flint glance down into the yard next door but the yard was empty.

"I'm up here."

Flint altered his gaze and discovered the three-year-old looking out the bathroom window on the second level of Jessie's house.

"Hey, Adam," Flint called back.

"I see'd you up there. I gotta go potty."

Flint laughed. "Okay, go ahead," he said for lack of anything else to say.

"Bye."

"Bye."

Flint went back to pounding nails into shingles and reminded himself of that other way that Jessie wasn't merely anyone else—with Jessie came four kids.

Four kids he had to factor in...

Marriage might be going from a sports car to a sedan, but add four kids to the picture and that was taking the leap all the way from sports car to minivan...

From childless bachelor to married man with children—it was daunting enough to give him pause.

Could he handle it?

He did like those kids, he admitted when he thought about it. Even Ella—who was still very lukewarm to him—was a sweetheart underneath her leeriness. And all the kids were similar to their mother in that they were strong and resilient and upbeat and funny and fun, too.

He was impressed by their outlook on things even after losing their father. And he got a kick out of their points of view, their senses of humor. He had a great time with them. And while he hadn't ever seen himself as a parent, he thought he'd done okay helping to give baths and put them to bed, looking after them on all of their outings. He'd even found himself feeling pretty protective of them along the way.

Granted none of that, none of the time he'd spent with Ella, Bethany, Braden and Adam amounted to much, but still, when he considered himself taking on that role, that, too, suddenly didn't seem so far-fetched. Especially not when he realized that Jessie's four kids were all little reflections of her and it occurred to him that because of that he couldn't help being smitten with them.

But having been a child of a single mother who had run numerous men through his life, Flint knew he couldn't take lightly the responsibility of being the man in Jessie's kids' lives. He couldn't risk disappointing those four kids if he couldn't do the dad bit wholeheartedly and with a solid commitment to be there for them for the distance. To literally be a father to them. A father they could count on as surely as they would have been able to count on their own dad.

Could he do that?

He gave it serious, solemn thought.

But the more he thought about it, the more he realized that he'd liked the times when the six of them had all been together almost as much as he'd liked the times he'd had Jessie to himself.

That he even liked what being with her kids brought out in him—a side of himself that he'd just discovered that made him not only able, but willing and eager to put them and their needs before his own. A side that he'd seen in Coop since Anthony had come into his brother's life. Another dimension that hadn't seemed like something he or Coop might actually have at their disposal before this.

But finding out that they did? Finding out that they

could be part of the Fortune family, and also finding out that they could be part of families of their own—even if it wasn't something that had ever seemed likely given the way they'd grown up themselves—was doubly nice.

"Fwint! I'm done!" Adam called from the bathroom window again.

"Good for you, big guy. Did you wash your hands?"

"I fuh-got."

"Do it now," Flint instructed, feeling very paternal and amused by that.

But somehow at that moment, it also occurred to him that what he'd said to Jessie when he'd told her about Myra was more true than he'd known at the time—he'd told Jessie that there were worse things than being a childless bachelor.

And suddenly it struck him that one of the things that was worse than being a childless bachelor would be to have come to know Jessie and her kids, and *go on* being a childless bachelor. To go on without them. Any of them.

So sign me up for the minivan, he thought.

"Okay, I dood it," Adam again yelled from the bathroom window a moment later.

"Good job!"

"Me an' Gramma an' Grampa an' all us kidses goin' to the store but Mama doan' wanna go. Do you wanna? 'Cuz you could come wis us if you did…"

"I think I'll have to pass, buddy. But you go on," Flint advised as the wheels began to spin even faster in his mind.

He wanted Jessie and he couldn't wait to let her know that. To hopefully hear her say that she wanted him, too. That she'd have him. That they could have a future together. That they could be a family.

He just couldn't wait...

They had plans to meet in the studio again tonight. But if everyone was going out and she'd be on her own now...

Be sure, he warned himself.

But he didn't really need to think any more about it to know that he was.

He was absolutely sure that he wanted Jessie.

Not for any reason except that he couldn't imagine his life without her.

Without her and everything that came with her.

Chapter Thirteen

Jessie was in her kitchen when Flint appeared at her back door.

She hadn't expected him, but that didn't keep her pulse from picking up speed the minute she set eyes on his handsome face, on his disheveled hair, on his disreputably sexy jeans and the simple chambray work shirt he wore untucked with the sleeves rolled to his elbows.

"Hey, beautiful, are you busy?" he asked through the screen in that deep voice that was music to her ears.

Jessie grinned at the *hey, beautiful* part, thinking that he was teasing her because her hair was in a ponytail, and she was wearing her oldest, most comfortable, but hardly best jeans, and the *World's Greatest Mom* T-shirt she'd had on the first day he'd arrived at Kelsey and Coop's.

"Just loading the dishwasher," she said, having finished that and closing the door to it as he opened the screen and came in without waiting for an invitation.

"A little birdy told me everyone over here was going to the store," he said, not hesitating to head directly for her and hook his arms around her waist.

"Well, not—"

He kissed her before she could finish saying that Ella had stayed behind to watch a Disney movie on DVD in the den.

And almost the moment his lips met hers the same thing happened that happened every time they were together now—everything faded into the background and Jessie was lost in Flint.

Her arms went around his neck and she clasped her hands behind it, knowing the silence of a kiss was not going to draw her eldest daughter away from the den and movie, and allowing herself that one secret mid-afternoon indulgence.

But she couldn't allow it for too long because it took nothing at all to arouse in her what Flint aroused night after night, and a clandestine kiss with her daughter in the next room was one thing; more than that just couldn't happen.

"Tonight," she reminded Flint when she ended the kiss. "Ella didn't go to the store. She's in the den."

Flint released her from his arms and stepped back, nodding his understanding. And smiling a smile that confused Jessie.

"I came to talk to you anyway," he said then.

A cold shiver ran up Jessie's spine.

She'd been blocking out the thought that he could be leaving anytime, that once his uncle's wedding on

Saturday was over, the logical assumption was that Flint would go back to Denver. And now she was afraid that that was what he wanted to talk about.

You knew it was going to happen, she told herself.

But while that was true, their nights alone in her studio had acted like a bubble of time, of space, that had encased just the two of them, together, and protected them from ugly realities.

But she thought the bubble was about to burst.

"Okay," she said quietly, tentatively, trying to keep the dread out of her voice. Trying also to be strong, to face this without showing how difficult it was for her.

"I don't know how you feel about—" he paused "—about us. But I've just realized some things—"

It took Jessie a moment to actually hear what he was saying, not to just be steeling herself for the blow she thought was coming.

And then an altogether different blow hit her when she actually began to absorb what he was saying.

He wasn't talking about returning to Colorado after the wedding the way she'd anticipated. He was talking about *not* returning to Colorado after the wedding. About staying in Red Rock. About staying with her. About them being together permanently.

"I think the website can cut my travel time way down," he was saying when she fully caught up with him. "I can rearrange things, too, so that the majority of the buying trips to accumulate inventory get done during the summer months, when the kids are out of school and we can make it like a big rock-hunting outing, except we'll be hunting for art and crafts. What sales trips have to happen beyond the summers I can do more efficiently. I've always taken my time, but there's no reason I can't get to where I'm going faster, piggyback meetings with buyers, and then be back before you've even missed me. Plus—"

"Wait…" Jessie said to slow him down. "Do you know what you're saying?"

He laughed. "I do. I'm saying that I'm so crazy about you, Jessie, that I can't even think about leaving you—"

"But with me comes *four* kids." Four kids she'd thought it unlikely for any man to ever want to take on, let alone a man like Flint. A man who was committed to being a bachelor because his only experiences with marriage had been abysmal. A man who had told her himself that he wasn't in favor of having kids, that he'd been terrified at the thought that Anthony might be his…

"I want the kids, too," he claimed enthusiastically, going on to tell her all he'd resolved about being a father to them.

"I want us to be a family," he swore. "I know I'm not the best at parenthood right now, that I kind of blunder my way through, but I'm not too horrible and I can learn. I'll get better at it. The most important part is that I *want* to be a father to your kids—"

"No!"

The shriek from the kitchen doorway drew both Jessie's and Flint's attention.

Jessie had been so astonished by all that Flint had been saying that she hadn't noticed that Ella had joined them. And she had no idea how long her daughter had been standing there, how much the little girl had overheard.

"Tell him no!" Ella commanded her mother.

"Ella—" Jessie cajoled.

"No!" the seven-year-old repeated. "He can't be our father. He's not a dad. He's not like Daddy, like Grampa. He's different. He'll get tired of us and he'll go away like Daddy did only worse. Daddy couldn't help going away. But him? He'll just go and then what will Adam do? What will Bethany and Braden do? They like him. They'll think he's our dad and then he'll go away and they'll cry and be sad like I was with Daddy. And you'll cry again, Mama. All the time, like over Daddy. Tell him no!"

Ella was sobbing by then and Jessie's eyes filled with tears to see it, to hear all that her daughter was worried about. And while letting things with Flint go as far as they had in the last several days had not been about her kids or about her being a mother, when it came to this much bigger issue, it was her children who took precedence.

"Ella," she said again, fighting her own tears and hating that she was going to have to turn down Flint this way, but knowing that Ella's feelings had to be her primary concern.

Yet before she had taken more than two steps toward her daughter, Flint said, "I understand, Ella." And he was the one to cross the kitchen to her daughter, where he hunkered down on his heels so he could be at Ella's eye level.

"I understand," he repeated, "that you're looking out for yourself, and for your brothers and sister, for your mom. My brother Ross always did that for me, for Coop, for our sister, Frannie. Ross was the oldest and he saw things the clearest, he knew when we needed protecting. So let's you and I talk."

"I just want you to go away," Ella cried.

"But what if I told you I want *never* to go away? That I know what it's like when you're a kid and you start to count on somebody, and how bad it is when they let you down?"

"How do you know?" she said venomously.

"Because it happened to me a whole bunch when I was growing up—that's how I know how bad it is. So I didn't come here today to say what I've said to your mom without knowing for sure that I want to come in here, with all of you, and be a dad to you in every way that being a dad means."

"You're not my dad."

"I know that. And I know that no one can ever take your own dad's place, and that's not what I'm trying to do. But what if you knew that if your mom said yes to me, you could count on me to always be here as your second dad? To be somebody you can always come to, who will always look out for you and Adam and Braden and Bethany the best way I know how? What if I promised you that I would never, ever leave any one of you willingly? Would it be such a bad thing to have me around then?"

Ella shrugged and Jessie could see that she was contemplating all that Flint had said, that she was wavering, and even though tears were still falling, she wasn't actively sobbing anymore.

"What if," he continued, "I told you that I don't want to take your mom away from any of you, that I just want you to share her with me? And that I'll do everything I can to make up for that by being with you guys myself? By doing the dad things with you all to fill in?"

"We have Grampa," she challenged.

"I know you do. And I'm not looking to take his place either. I'm just looking to be a part of what you all have here. Would that be so bad? To just have us all be a family?"

Ella's tears stopped, but the sniffles remained and she was having trouble keeping her bottom lip from jutting out. "Would we still have game night and go rock hunting and all the stuff we like to do with Mama?"

"You would."

"But you'd be there."

"If you—and your mom—will let me, I'd like to be, yeah."

"Would you holler at us?"

"I'd like to say no, but there would probably be times when I'd get mad at something, just like there would probably be times when you would get mad at me. But there are times when that happens with your mom, too, aren't there? And with your gramma and grampa? Times when your dad got mad?"

Ella shrugged her concession to that.

"I'll tell you what, though. I know what you're talking about and I know how it felt when the man in my mother's life yelled at me or did something that made me angry, so I can also promise you that when that happens, you and I can talk about it. That you can tell me how you feel and we can see what we can do to make everything be the best it can be for everybody. Is that something you think you might be able to live with?"

"And you won't just go away if we're bad?"

"I won't. I'll stay and we'll make it work. I give you my word."

He said that so solemnly that that, too, broke Jessie's heart and brought tears to her eyes as she looked on, as she watched her daughter study Flint, as she watched Flint endure that scrutiny that seemed to be Ella searching for signs that he was lying.

Only after a long while did Jessie see Ella swallow hard, pull in her bottom lip once and for all, and say, "Okay, I guess." Then, to Jessie, the seven-year-old said, "You can marry him."

"He hasn't actually asked me to marry him," Jessie pointed out, realizing that the ball was suddenly in her court again and not instantly sure what she was going to do about it.

"Why don't you go back to your movie and let me have a few minutes alone with her?" Flint said to Ella as if they were now in this together.

Ella still wasn't smiling. She was still clearly leery even if she had conceded. And before she conceded enough to leave, the front door opened and in came Jack and Jeannie and the rest of the kids.

"What's going on?" Jeannie asked as she took in the wet, red face of her eldest granddaughter and then looked from Flint as he stood up from his stance in front of Ella to Jessie.

"Mama and Flint are gonna get married," Ella announced somewhat fatalistically.

"We're just talking!" Jessie was very quick to interject.

"Maybe we can go on doing that in the studio," Flint suggested.

"Will you guys keep an eye on the kids?" Jessie asked her obviously shocked parents.

They agreed and without waiting for more, Flint took Jessie's hand and led her out the back door.

What am I going to do? Tell me what to do, Pete…

Jessie was in a panic as she crossed the yard with Flint. But when they reached her studio Flint had to stop to answer a call to him by Coop from over the fence and she went in without him, grateful for even a minute to herself to think.

But somehow once she was in her studio, where they'd spent every night, where her life seemed to have taken yet another change, a calm came over her.

Or maybe it was Pete bringing that calm over her because again she had the sense of his presence. But not in any way that relayed displeasure. Not even in any way that caused her to feel disloyal. Instead, if anything, she somehow felt as if she had his approval along with Ella's...

"Pete?" she whispered because the sense of him was so strong that she wasn't sure if she was having some sort of hallucination.

But of course nothing happened. Nothing but a continuing feeling that everything was okay. And then that sense of him went away, as if he'd left her to her thoughts, to make her own decision freely.

And yes, she thought she had a decision to make because, like Ella, she, too, had had the impression that all Flint had said was leading to a proposal. Having a future together, being a family, never leaving them. What else could he have been talking about except marriage?

But *marry* him?

Her mother had encouraged her to have this time with him while he was in Red Rock, this brief interlude, to indulge herself, to just enjoy what he had to offer. And she'd done that. To the hilt. And no, she hadn't wanted to so much as entertain the thought of his leaving. But in the back of her mind, she also hadn't doubted that he would.

But now...

What if he didn't? What if she *could* have more than this passing fancy with him? What if she *could* have an entire future with him?

It was surprisingly simple to consider.

Her mother had been right in all of her observations of Jessie's response to Flint—she had gravitated toward him from the start, he did make her laugh, she did enjoy him. Every minute with him. Everything about him.

And what Jessie had said herself was also true—she was more comfortable with him than she'd ever been with anyone other than Pete. But more than comfortable, during these last nights together—working together, talking, joking and teasing, then drawing closer and closer, kissing, touching, making love—none of that had been merely about being comfortable with Flint. There was so much more to what she found with him. What she felt about him. For him.

And now, potentially, that could go on.

She could have Flint. Night *and* day.

Elation came with that thought. But even so, she was very aware that it wasn't for herself alone that she would be making that decision, that there were the kids to consider.

Yes, Flint had basically won over Ella in the end. And Jessie knew that Adam, Braden and Bethany would be thrilled because Adam adored Flint, and even the twins were already more than fond of him. But was making Flint a permanent fixture in their lives best for them?

Flint didn't come from a stable background. His own history wasn't stellar. And she again recalled that he'd defended his bachelorhood and been clear about his lack of desire to have kids.

None of that added up to the ideal guy to bring into her family.

And yet...

Coop had come from the same background and had had a similar commitment to being a loner, and he'd settled in just fine with Kelsey and Anthony. And more importantly, he loved it. He loved them.

So maybe history could be overcome. Especially when the desire to put it behind was there. And certainly from what Flint had said in the kitchen, he had the desire to move on. To move on to her. To being a father to her kids. He'd even promised Ella that he would always be there for her...

Jessie considered that promise, she weighed whether Flint would make good on it.

But she discovered that she didn't doubt that if he made a promise, he would keep it because he was a man who did what he said he was going to do. He'd proven that with the commitment he'd made to Kelsey and Coop to help with their house, he'd proven it with her in what he'd already done with her sculptures.

And what he'd done with her sculptures also made her think about his unfailing support of her, of her work, his encouragement, his belief in her. It made her think about how he saw her as more than the mother of four. He saw her as herself, too, as a person, as a woman— that had helped her to see herself in those lights again as well, and that was of more value to her than he could ever know.

Everything he'd brought into her life was of value, she realized. His patience, his humor, his easygoing nature, his strength and willingness to pitch in, to help, to bear some of the burden. But with all he'd brought into her life, with the way he made her feel, with the way she felt about him, came the risk that she could lose it all, too—despite his promise that he wouldn't go anywhere.

That was a promise Pete would have kept if he could have, too.

Okay, yes, there was that lingering fear—that even if she trusted Flint not to leave of his own volition, she could still lose him. Her kids could still lose him.

And if she allowed Flint into her life more than he already was? Into her kids' lives? And then they lost him? Could she—could her kids—go through that again?

It would be devastating. And horrible. And nothing she would ever—*ever*—want any of them to have to go through again.

But she came to the conclusion that the only way to be absolutely certain that she and her kids never suffered a loss as severe as the loss of Pete was to never let anyone get as close as Pete had been. Which would mean saying no to Flint. Closing that door forever.

And suddenly the image of that, of returning to the way things had been in the last two years, wasn't one that Jessie wanted to entertain. Flint had already added so much to her life, and even to the lives of her kids in small ways like the thoughtful gifts he'd given them with each of their personalities and problems in mind. He added an element that not even having her parents live with them had replaced with the loss of Pete. An element that was all his own.

To lose that even now wasn't something she wanted to go through. It wasn't something she wanted her kids to go through.

Life was full of risks, she decided. Was she going to throw away what she had, what she could have, what she wanted, in an attempt to keep those risks to a minimum?

That seemed like a very fearful way to live. And not something she wanted to teach her kids as they went on to live their own lives, make their own decisions. When they faced the need to take risks themselves, she didn't want fear to be what ruled them. So she couldn't let fear be what ruled her now.

Flint finally came through the studio door and closed it behind him. Then he turned the lock and leaned against the wooden panel as if to barricade it.

That was when he laughed and shook his head. "What were we talking about?" he joked as if it hadn't been memorable.

Jessie laughed, too, taking in the sight of him, knowing in that moment that despite the fact that she'd thought she would never be able to love anyone the way she'd loved Pete, she felt every bit as much for Flint. That her feelings for him were stronger than all of her fears put together, stronger even than her feelings of disloyalty had been.

"I believe there was some talk about the future…" she said.

"Oh, yeah, right," he pretended that his memory had been jogged. "I was about to say that I'm madly in love with you, Jessie, and ask you to be my wife."

"Simple as that? No fanfare?"

"I was afraid if I didn't get it out as soon as I could we might have more interruptions," he joked again.

He pushed away from the door and came to stand in front of her, clasping her arms in his big hands, squeezing as he gazed down into her eyes. Then he abandoned all teasing to repeat in a quiet, solemn tone of voice, "I love you, Jess. More than I ever thought it was possible to love anyone. I want you to be my wife. I want to be your husband. I want to be a father to your kids. Will you marry me?"

"I will," she answered as if it hadn't taken any thought, any struggle to get her there. "I will because I love you, too, Flint."

He smiled a poignant, heartfelt smile just before he kissed her, sweetly, chastely.

But there was always too much heat between them for it to stay sweet or chaste, and after a few moments his lips parted, that kiss deepened and daylight or no daylight, what erupted was what had erupted so many times already in that studio.

The most Jessie paid attention to beyond Flint was to make sure the curtains were pulled closed over the windows. When she was reassured that they were, clothes began to come off and hands went on familiar adventures that instantly aroused and fed desires in her that had grown by leaps and bounds since learning what Flint had to teach.

Naked and uninhibited, they ended up on the sofa where it had all begun that other night, mouths hungrily meeting, then fleeing to seek out other parts to delight and tease and awaken to new and old sensations.

Hands trailed paths of divine pleasure, too, until neither of them could contain themselves a moment more. Bodies moved together to form one. Striving for that climax that always blinded them both in pure, exquisite ecstasy. That climax that held them so sublimely that nothing could penetrate it until they were spent and sated and Jessie knew all over again that being with that man for the rest of her life was exactly what she wanted.

"It's the middle of the afternoon," she reminded when she could, when she'd caught her breath and was almost too weak to care. "After what Ella told my parents you know that they called Kelsey and told her something was going on. So the whole crew is probably watching this place and just waiting for us to come out. And look what you made me do," she concluded as if she were blameless.

She was on top, lying with her head on Flint's chest, listening to his heart beat. She tilted her head backward to look up at him. To see the smile she was sure would be on his handsome face.

"Yep," he agreed. "I'm bad. But you?" He groaned a deep-throated, sexy groan. "You are sooo good it's worth it."

Jessie laughed. "But your punishment is going to be no nap. If we don't get out of here soon, you can bet someone is going to come knocking. And I don't want to be found like this."

"We'll just say the honeymoon started a little early."

"We'll say that to my mother, my father, my sister and my children?"

"Hmm, yeah, I suppose those are not the people to say it to."

After another moment of reveling in afterglow and just being naked in his arms, Jessie sighed and got up. "We'll also have to look presentable," she informed him gathering her clothes.

"Then I can sleep for ten minutes while you fuss because all I have to do is pull on my clothes."

Jessie playfully hit him with one of the throw pillows that had fallen off the couch.

But she spent a minute watching him drift off, loving that sight as much as she loved everything else about him.

Then it occurred to her that from here on she would have that same face to look at whenever she wanted to.

As she headed for the bathroom to make it appear that she hadn't just been made love to, the thought of the years, the life with Flint that stretched out ahead of her filled her with more joy than she'd ever thought to feel again.

Joy she couldn't wait to share with her family.

And with Flint's family.

Which they would be able to do; in a few minutes they could share it with her parents, her sister, her kids, his brother.

Then the day after tomorrow, they could share it with the rest of the Fortune family at William and Lily's wedding.

No, taking those first steps, announcing their intention to spend the rest of their lives together, wasn't quite as wonderful as it would have been to be still lying in Flint's arms at that moment.

But they were steps she wanted to take.

Because taking them would put a formal seal on what she knew in her heart would be a phase as perfect for the second portion of her life as Pete had been for the last.

Epilogue

"Thank you all for coming early."

That was how William got the attention of the male members of his family a mere fifteen minutes before his wedding to Lily was to begin.

Flint was standing in the church basement between Ross and Coop. Around them were their cousins—William's sons—Drew, Jeremy, Darr, Nicholas and JR, as well as twenty-year-old Josh, who was the son of Frannie and Roberto Mendoza, making him Ross, Coop and Flint's nephew and William's great-nephew.

Everyone—including underage Josh—had been handed a glass of champagne as they'd come into the church basement.

"I have something to say and I have three toasts to make," William continued. "First of all, Drew—" William focused his attention on that particular son "—I want you to know that I'm now ready to pass the reins of Fortune Forecasting on to you. With my memory as good as new, I can tell you that my only intention in delaying my retirement before was to make sure that work was not the only thing you ended up having in life. But now that you and Deanna have found each other just the way I was hoping—and trying to make sure—you would—"

Everyone laughed along with William and raised their glasses in agreement with that sentiment.

"Now that you and Deanna have found each other and tied the knot, I know that you will have what I wanted you to have, and that I can step down and enjoy the years I have left focusing only on Lily, knowing the business will be in the best hands it could be in."

Congratulations were extended by everyone—to Drew for becoming the CEO of Fortune Forecasting, and to William for his retirement.

But as Flint glanced at his cousin he thought that Drew was taking in stride having finally achieved what had once upon a time been the only thing he'd strived for.

Now he has Deanna and she's more important...

That was what flashed through Flint's mind, but it was what he believed—that his cousin had discovered that Deanna meant more to him than any job or any promotion.

"I want to toast my cousin Ryan," William held his glass high and glanced upward, above everyone's heads. "I miss you. Lily misses you. But we both hope you're here with us today in spirit, giving us your blessing. And I want you to know that I will take good care of our Lily, knowing full well that she always has a place in her heart for you."

"To Ryan," everyone echoed.

William lowered his glass and his glance to his sons, his nephews, his great-nephew, and Flint felt a swell of pride to be included in this.

"And last but not least, I toast you all—the Fortune men. The Fortune family. *My* family. I'm proud of each and every one of you. I'm grateful for each and every one of you. And I wish each and every one of you the same happiness that I've found with Lily, who today I will—a little late—get to make my wife. To you all—health, happiness, love!"

All glasses were raised, clinked with any that were nearby, and then the champagne was sipped a third time.

"And to you, Dad," JR said then. "To you and Lily, to getting your memory back, to many, many years to come."

"Hear, hear!" Darr seconded and then that toast, too, was supported all around before the champagne was polished off.

Then, setting his glass down with some ceremony, William raised instead a brilliant smile and said, "Now, let me go get married!"

Jessie had no idea what the first, unsuccessful wedding of Lily and William Fortune might have been like, but as she sat beside Flint and her children in the church, she couldn't imagine that it would have been any more beautiful, any more heartfelt, any more touching than the ceremony that joined them Saturday evening.

But once the groom had kissed his bride and Jessie

expected them to leave the altar, they instead turned to face their guests, both of them smiling as William said, "We have a surprise. For those of you who might not know one or the other of these people, let me introduce them as they come up here—my son Jeremy and his fiancée, Kirsten Allen. And my nephew Cooper Fortune and Kelsey Hunt…"

Confused, Jessie glanced at Flint for clarification, but he looked as puzzled as she was and merely shrugged.

When both couples had stepped onto the altar with William and Lily, William said, "We've seen the marriages of two other couples in the last few months—my son Drew and the former Deanna Gurney, and Rafe Mendoza and Melina Lawrence—and now these other two couples have asked to do Lily and I the honor of sharing this special day with us by making it their wedding day, too."

A ripple of shock ran through the church and William waited for it to settle again. Then he said, "Don't worry, this has been in the works since shortly after Lily and I set this new date, so marriage licenses have been granted, the waiting period has been met and it's all legal. And now if you'll sit tight, Lily and I are going to get to be witness to these wonderful joinings…"

So, with Flint holding her hand, Jessie watched as her sister married his brother, as the other couple had their own moments, and then there were two more pronouncements of man and wife.

With that, protocol went out the window. Close family members of all three couples rushed to hug them, to shake their hands, to congratulate and chastise them for keeping secrets before wishing them all the best.

Then everyone filed into the church basement for the reception that celebrated not one wedding but three.

During the course of the reception several people stopped the dance music to offer best wishes, so Jessie wasn't surprised when Flint did that as well, when he disappeared from her side for the first time and reappeared to stand at the microphone.

As had happened with the other interruptions, everyone paused their dance or their conversations and turned to face him, including Jessie, who was standing near the table her family had occupied for dinner, where the kids and her parents were eating cake.

Flint first offered some teasing of the newly married couples, some joking about mass marriages, then added his congratulations to the lot. "And I'd also like to congratulate our delegate from the Atlanta branch of the Fortune family—Wendy—and her fiancé, Marcos Mendoza. Wendy came to Red Rock looking for a career and found Marcos instead, and they just told us that they're expecting a baby!"

Hoots and hollers accompanied applause and more calls of congratulations along with a few jibes about getting as much sleep as they could in the months to come.

And then, when that wave of elation died down, Flint said, "Last but certainly not least, I also have an announcement of my own to make."

Flint's eyes met Jessie's and he smiled warmly at her for a long moment before he switched his gaze to the crowd of onlookers.

"Although it seems impossible that anyone would have me," he said, making everyone laugh, "the abundantly generous and undeniably gorgeous Jessie Hunt-Myers and her very, very fine children—Ella..." He tossed the seven-year-old a wink and when Jessie glanced at her daughter sitting closest to where she was standing she discovered that Ella was blushing but smiling in delight. "Bethany, Braden and Adam, have agreed to marry me, too."

"Mama, he says he's marrying us all..." Ella whispered to Jessie amidst yet another round of clapping, cheering, congratulations and jests.

"Well, I guess he is," Jessie said to her daughter, seeing that that fact pleased Ella.

"We haven't decided exactly where or when yet," Flint continued, "but it'll be soon. The sooner the better as far as I'm concerned," he said more to Jessie than to the group. "But whenever and wherever it happens, you're all invited to the wedding!"

Then he stepped from behind the microphone and came directly to Jessie to take her into his arms and kiss her while applause surrounded them.

The music and dancing resumed, and when their kiss ended Flint gazed into her eyes and said for her ears only, "I do love you, Jess. There aren't enough words for how much."

"I love you, too," she told him, her heart swollen with feelings for him.

"But I promised Ella this dance," he confided.

"Go ahead," she said, thrilled that her eldest daughter was now welcoming him.

As Jessie watched the man she truly did love with all her heart take her seven-year-old onto the dance floor she knew that not only had she and her kids found a new lease on happiness, but so had the rest of the Fortune family.

And suddenly her gaze caught on the framed photograph of Ryan Fortune that was displayed near the wedding cake as a way to include William's late cousin, Lily's late husband in the festivities. Much as she sometimes thought she could sense Pete's presence, she had the strongest feeling at that moment that it was Ryan Fortune who was there this time, looking down over it all.

Over his dearly loved widow, Lily, who was now in the arms of her new husband, William.

Over his nieces and nephews and friends who had all somehow found paths to people who seemed exactly right for them.

Over baby Anthony who had made his way into the Fortune family through no easy road, but who offered an entirely new generation of Fortunes to continue the name, the legacy.

And without any explanation for it, Jessie had the sense that the late Ryan Fortune could finally move on.

And maybe, just maybe the breath of the breeze that brushed through the room just then, as Jessie answered Flint's motion for her to join him and Ella on the dance floor, was one last kiss that Ryan blew to Lily.

To the Fortunes one and all.

Before he said goodbye.

* * * * *

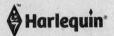
Harlequin®

COMING NEXT MONTH
Available June 28, 2011

SPECIAL EDITION

REQUEST YOUR FREE BOOKS!

2 FREE NOVELS PLUS 2 FREE GIFTS!

SPECIAL EDITION

Life, Love & Family

YES! Please send me 2 FREE Harlequin Special Edition® novels and my 2 FREE gifts (gifts are worth about $10). After receiving them, if I don't wish to receive any more books, I can return the shipping statement marked "cancel." If I don't cancel, I will receive 6 brand-new novels every month and be billed just $4.24 per book in the U.S. or $4.99 per book in Canada. That's a saving of at least 15% off the cover price! It's quite a bargain! Shipping and handling is just 50¢ per book in the U.S. and 75¢ per book in Canada.* I understand that accepting the 2 free books and gifts places me under no obligation to buy anything. I can always return a shipment and cancel at any time. Even if I never buy another book, the two free books and gifts are mine to keep forever.

235/335 SDN FC7H

Name	(PLEASE PRINT)

Address	Apt. #

City	State/Prov.	Zip/Postal Code

Signature (if under 18, a parent or guardian must sign)

Mail to the **Reader Service**:
IN U.S.A.: P.O. Box 1867, Buffalo, NY 14240-1867
IN CANADA: P.O. Box 609, Fort Erie, Ontario L2A 5X3

Not valid for current subscribers to Harlequin Special Edition books.

Want to try two free books from another line?
Call 1-800-873-8635 or visit www.ReaderService.com.

* Terms and prices subject to change without notice. Prices do not include applicable taxes. Sales tax applicable in N.Y. Canadian residents will be charged applicable taxes. Offer not valid in Quebec. This offer is limited to one order per household. All orders subject to credit approval. Credit or debit balances in a customer's account(s) may be offset by any other outstanding balance owed by or to the customer. Please allow 4 to 6 weeks for delivery. Offer available while quantities last.

Your Privacy—The Reader Service is committed to protecting your privacy. Our Privacy Policy is available online at www.ReaderService.com or upon request from the Reader Service.

We make a portion of our mailing list available to reputable third parties that offer products we believe may interest you. If you prefer that we not exchange your name with third parties, or if you wish to clarify or modify your communication preferences, please visit us at www.ReaderService.com/consumerschoice or write to us at Reader Service Preference Service, P.O. Box 9062, Buffalo, NY 14269. Include your complete name and address.

USA TODAY *bestselling author B.J. Daniels*
takes you on a trip to Whitehorse, Montana,
and the Chisholm Cattle Company.

RUSTLED

Available July 2011 from Harlequin Intrigue.

As the dust settled, Dawson got his first good look at the rustler. A pair of big Montana sky-blue eyes glared up at him from a face framed by blond curls.

A woman rustler?

"You have to let me go," she hollered as the roar of the stampeding cattle died off in the distance.

"So you can finish stealing my cattle? I don't think so." Dawson jerked the woman to her feet.

She reached for the gun strapped to her hip hidden under her long barn jacket.

He grabbed the weapon before she could, his eyes narrowing as he assessed her. "How many others are there?" he demanded, grabbing a fistful of her jacket. "I think you'd better start talking before I tear into you."

She tried to fight him off, but he was on to her tricks and pinned her to the ground. He was suddenly aware of the soft curves beneath the jean jacket she wore under her coat.

"You have to listen to me." She ground out the words from between her gritted teeth. "You have to let me go. If you don't they will come back for me and they will kill you. There are too many of them for you to fight off alone. You won't stand a chance and I don't want your blood on my hands."

"I'm touched by your concern for me. Especially after you just tried to pull a gun on me."

HIEXP0711R

"I wasn't going to shoot you."

Dawson hauled her to her feet and walked her the rest of the way to his horse. Reaching into his saddlebag, he pulled out a length of rope.

"You can't tie me up."

He pulled her hands behind her back and began to tie her wrists together.

"If you let me go, I can keep them from coming back," she said. "You have my word." She let out an unladylike curse. "I'm just trying to save your sorry neck."

"And I'm just going after my cattle."

"Don't you mean your boss's cattle?"

"Those cattle are mine."

"*You're* a Chisholm?"

"Dawson Chisholm. And you are…?"

"Everyone calls me Jinx."

He chuckled. "I can see why."

*Bronco busting, falling in love…it's all in a day's work.
Look for the rest of their story in*

RUSTLED

*Available July 2011 from Harlequin Intrigue
wherever books are sold.*